# Praise for Pantheon

**Eric Syrdal's *Pantheon* takes readers on an epic journey through time, space, and emotion.**

Syrdal, a self-proclaimed romantic and sci-fi and fantasy enthusiast, does not disappoint: He deftly weaves a tale of adventure, his protagonists crossing paths with virtuous Goddesses, who coax them toward their destinies.

As I read the first section, I worried that *Pantheon* was a little too heavy on the usual themes of fantasy and fairy tale: Warhorses champing at the bit, armored fighters, swords at the ready, the proverbial dragon looming over the embattled heroic Poet. Despite this, I continued on and was glad I did, for Syrdal quickly demonstrates that his story stands apart from, and above, the typical. With Courage and the Queen of Hearts at his side, and Hope, Grace, Mercy, Karma and Fate in the shadows, the Poet must make a pivotal decision. His choice at that critical moment is masterfully mirrored in the subsequent sections of the book, and I marveled time and again at the way Syrdal coherently connected his multiple story lines, the seams necessarily apparent but still flawless.

*Pantheon* finishes as epically as it began. All along, the Queen of Hearts and her sisters have artfully molded their heroes' journeys, bringing them back to central truths about life and love. Should you read this book (and you should!), I trust that the imagery of that final section will be long lasting in your mind, along with a sense of awe at Syrdal's beautifully written verse and sense of literary craftsmanship.

—Mariah Voutilainen, *Indie Blu(e)*

*"When the ones I protect are worth less than my own life"*
*"If gods and goddesses/ look down on our lives"*

There is nothing unoriginal about this novel, it's just a gripping, incredible tour de force and explosive, emotive, classic that I believe will continue to take the indie market by storm. To try to describe it would take far too long, think Neil Gaiman on ecstasy and set on fire by starlight and you may be close.

If it is your desire to read something astoundingly original, from a writer who is not only a truly breathtaking author, deft with supernatural words and ideas, but a dreamer of worlds, who will blow any preconceived notions you have away and leave you shell shocked by the sheer power of his mind, then I cannot recommend Eric Syrdal and his novel *Pantheon* more highly. *"I built this beach / and the stars / and the moon .... I turn back the wheels of heaven / and make time stop and rewind / over and over ..... Because I don't know how to tell him / A machine had a wish."*

—Candice Louisa Daquin, author of *Pinch the Lock*

**I found myself sitting for three hours, empty coffee cups scattered around me, utterly absorbed in the storytelling and the crafting of language.**

"The poetry is densely colourful, rich in imagery and sensuality, boldly imaginative and deeply sensitive to the human condition, while being written with clarity and emotional pull.

Syrdal has created something very powerful, using elements of history, science fiction, worldly fantasy and unmistakable reality to bind these pieces together in a system of belief and fantastic-theology that appears utterly believable, utterly intoxicating."

—Lois E. Linkens

***Pantheon*'s author, Eric Syrdal, has written an updated epic that would make the likes of Homer to Gene Roddenberry proud as it spans across time and space, quite literally.**

Utilizing a pantheon of goddesses as reoccurring motifs, we are treated to the personification of Hope, Courage, Fate, and more. Not only do they serve as a literal guide for our poet, but for each and every one of us. But beyond bold and beautiful deities, there are also great monsters and fierce battles reminiscent of Beowulf. Their symbolism is woven throughout the expansive narrative. In one story, our hero is in medieval times, and another, a contemporary coffee shop, but both of them are fighting their own dragons. What I marvel at most, however, is when Syrdal's verses travel to space. I love a good genre blend, and seeing his pantheon transcend to a time that has moved on from mysticism is truly epic.

Syrdal's prose itself is beautiful and trim of fat. The occasional long stanzas are ripe with emotion. They hit home and linger between fast staccatos of verses that push along not only description and dialogue, but urgency, too. The literal and figurative are also maximized for an evocative response. At times, I found myself tearing up, and that's rare for me. But the biggest achievement, in my opinion, is making poetry as riveting as it is beautiful. *Pantheon* is truly an adventure to read, accessible for today's audiences who love fantasy, science fiction, and above all else, soul.

Eric Syrdal is a talented wordsmith with his heart as his forge. Indulge in his craft. You won't be disappointed.

—Larysia Writes, *Blogspot*

# PANTHEON

ERIC SYRDAL

Havertown, Pennsylvania

Pantheon
Copyright © 2020 Eric Syrdal



For information, address
Indie Blu(e) Publishing.
indieblucollective@gmail.com
Published in the United States of America
by Indie Blu(e) Publishing

ISBN 978-1-7328000-8-3
Library of Congress Control Number: 2020936869

Editors:        Christine E. Ray
                Kindra M. Austin
Cover Design:   Mitch Green

## DEDICATION

For my family and friends
for Aimee, Sarah and Nicholas
for Tami Hadley and her term papers
for Sarah Brentyn and her faith in my work
for Maria Barrett, Sister New Orleanian and beloved ally

## ACKNOWLEDGEMENTS

Special thanks to Kindra M. Austin; Christine E. Ray; Mitch Green; Candice Daquin; and Indie Blu(e) Publishing, who have made a dream come true.

# Table of Contents

# PANTHEON

Eric Syrdal

# BACK TO THE BEGINNING...

I awake to
weighted silence
flat on my back
The sky has turned
to the soft pink and orange
of sunset

I am covered in blood
Mine or theirs?
I do not hear the roar
of the mob

I see her face over me
Grace extends a slender-fingered
dark skinned hand
With the strength of a titan
she lifts me to my feet

Soon I am face to face with her
dark eyes, framed in tight black curls
She releases me only when I have steadied
my balance

To my left stands Karma
She steps closer
With no more effort than a child
would handle a beloved toy,
she returns my shield to my arm

There is an innocence in her
fluid way
Her hazel eyes contrast

Pantheon

Her auburn hair
To my right, Fate
covers my shoulders in
cool linen cloth
Gently draping against wounds
I thought had long since closed

Golden-haired, emerald-eyed
mistress of the forge
Nothing that should be or will be
comes into this world except by her skilled hands

I turn to face Mercy
she stands at arm's length
Her beauty blots out the sun
I close my eyes in her shadow
as the edge comes off the pain

Her brown eyes are filled with tears as
she touches a delicate hand to my cheek
Holding it tenderly
My sanguine eyes beg the question
But she whispers softly, *"Not today, Love"*

She steps aside
and gestures that I may pass
I acknowledge her words
with a rasping breath
and a compliant nod

As I begin to take a step
Courage moves beside me
Her cobalt blue eyes tell me a story
of when I was little
She takes my hand in hers

I feel it lift to her face
She presses her lips against the back

She has never minded the blood, or the sand, or the scars

and together we walk

…back to the beginning.

# **PANTHEON: QUEEN OF HEARTS**

I heard the hoof beats from miles away
behind me
heard it when they left the paved road
thundering over the open ground
deep breaths of air
filling her mount's lungs

A powerful ebony draft horse

A living war machine that
carried her to victory in countless engagements
ribbons of scarlet woven into its mane
amid the clicks and jingles of tack and harness

I hear the clamor of steel plates
she's donned her armor for this visit
no popping of the battle standard
her entourage is not at her flank
the smell of cloves and orange blossom
carried to me by the wind at her back

She did not come to fight
When she does
she smells of leather oil and Greek pitch
I slow my pace as I amble on

Dear gods, even in my fury
I accommodate her;

Her mount slows to a canter

As she draws up alongside me

I keep my eyes fixed on the path
once our eyes meet, I am finished
She paces the warhorse to meet my own
Several heartbeats pass without a word
I can hear the equine breathing;
it's labored as the creature tries to send
vital oxygen rich blood to its quivering muscles

I am not foolish enough to believe this moment will pass smoothly

*"Where are you going?"*

"To work"

*"Yours, Hers, Theirs?"*

"Yes" I reply, I can hear her tongue move to the inside of her cheek
in frustration.

*"When are you going to learn you can't lie to me?"*

"When the ones I protect are worth less than my own life"

*"So **never** then?"*

"In the language of my country, I believe that is the right term. Your
Majesty"
*"Don't call me that! Do you mock me, poet?"*

"Never, My Lady"

In my periphery, she pulls back on the reins.
The warhorse nods its head, with a puff of air, in agreement with me.

*"You left your blade at home."*

"I did."

*"Don't you need it?"*

"No. Where are your sisters? Are they not concerned for your safety out here?"

*"I left them behind some days ago. They are looking after Hope. She is not well."*

I stop in my tracks,
causing her to bring her mount to a halt.
The warhorse protests with a stamp of a massive hoof.
I take a deep breath, and continue walking
And she resumes her escort.

*"She does so poorly when you are gone so long."*

"I'm busy."

She clicks her tongue against her bottom teeth, *"I see you remembered your aegis."*

As I am reminded of it now, it seems so heavy on my arm,
suddenly becoming cast iron.
I heft it back into position and offer no reply.

*"You've forgotten how to use it."*

"I have not." I offer, feeling heat rise to the back of my neck.

*"Yes, you have. You forget, I am with you in the arena. I see what you do. I've watched you deflect flea bites that would cause us no more harm than a baby's breath. Yet, let through wounds that would stagger my horse."*

"Tactics..." I retort.

*"Excuses..."* she sighs.

With a mighty bellow, I turn sharply and muster all my strength to
hurl the shield well beyond our reach.
It takes a bite out of the earth and rolls on its edge in a complete
circle before thudding to rest in the tall grass.

My outburst brings her to a stop and silence passes for what feels like
years.
The only sound is the echo of my scream and the breathing of her
horse.

I feel, more than hear
her fidget in the saddle.
Her voice is restrained.
She is furious.

*"Why don't you look at me?"*

"Because you are too beautiful."

A polite chuckle, *"You have made me so. You and your stories of our
experiences. The collection of you inside me...each box and file
cabinet filled with dreams. Fairy tales. Like Sleeping Beauty."*

"It has nothing to do with Beauty."

*"No, it doesn't. Does it? It's only ever Philip and Maleficent. The
black thorns around the castle. Defeating the dragon. Green flames
and all. You never climb the tower."*
"That's not my part of the story."

Pantheon

*"How long? How long have we been out here in the black thorns?*
*How many dragons have we sent to their rest?"*

"They always come back."

*"Because you never climb the tower. Courage was with you last time.*
*She told you to do it. And you—"*

"I sent her back to you."

She sighs heavily and I hear the creaking of her leather as she climbs
down from her mount.
I imagine I can keep my eyes focused on the ground
as she ducks under the muscular neck of her horse
and makes her way to my shield.

With one hand she plucks it from the ground and begins to move in
my direction.
With every atom of my being I struggle against the pull of her.
But my eyes won't be convinced.
So, as she stands before me, they surrender to her image.

She is a half hand taller than myself.
Her armor is fashioned of a metal
which shines blood red in the morning sun.

Following her, combing the dew covered weeds
a train of deep burgundy moves behind her steps
Her skin, so pale, shows freckles
around her sweet face.
Her hair, deepest amber, lies flowing on her shoulders
instead of pulled back into the tight woven plait I am used to.
On her head a resplendent tiara glittering golden and bright.

But her eyes
softest blue
like the snow reflecting the sky on the mountains.
They are the hardest of all to avoid.

I can feel my knees wanting to bend.
But I plant my feet firmly.

She holds my shield out

As I take it with both hands, she smiles at me

*"Returned, forthwith, to the only master it has ever known."*

She waits patiently as I affix it in place and then,
to my distress, she takes my other hand into her own
She extends my arm and places my hand against her cheek
and then closes her eyes
pressing her face against my palm.

*"You never touch me anymore."* Her voice is almost a whisper and
the world around us instantly quiets so I can hear her.

"I'm afraid."

*"Of what, My Love?"*

"Of you…"

*"Why?"*

Just then my eyes find the exposed skin above her breastplate.

Near the base of her neck, there is a massive wound.

Pantheon

A deep bite from a blade.
Angry. Red, purple, and blue.

"My Lady, I..." my voice breaks.

*"It's nothing. Don't worry about it."*

"Like hell it is." I counter

*"Answer me, Love. Why are you afraid?"*

"I'm afraid you'll die."

*"Not as long as you remember, you made me more powerful than this. You built me the most beautiful palace to live in."*

"It is old and drafty."

*"No more so than in the last lifetime."* She opens her eyes and gently moves my hand to her mouth, placing a delicate kiss in my palm. She looks deep into my eyes.

"Its walls are useless."

*"They glitter in the sun when I live there."* She closes my fingers over my palm and presses my fist back into the center of my own chest. *"When will you learn that we can do so much more together than when we are apart? So much more, when I am standing next to you on that battle line than when I stand opposed to your cause? But I cannot live in this glorious palace"* She gestures to my chest, *"when it wanders so far away from me."*

"I don't want to see some of the things you show me."
She nods and indicates a quill pen sticking from my back pocket, *"Yet you use this to write down the deepest of my memories?"*

I nod, suddenly flushing with the heat of embarrassment.

*"Because that is who you are.  Who WE are…"* Her hand releases my fist and moves back to her side as she turns to head back to her mount.

I follow her
gathering up her train…holding the reins
while she climbs back into the saddle.

I make sure her feet are planted firmly in the stirrups
smoothing out the burgundy cloth across the back of her horse
as I return the reins to her strong hands, she is the picture of regal
splendor

The sun glints off of her tiara causing me to shield my eyes
A breeze lifts some of the hair from beside her face as she smiles
down at me

*"Don't be too long…"* she sighs, *"Brave warrior."*

"I won't, My Lady."

*"You are needed back where we belong. We have much to do! And the battle will be hard."*

"I understand."

*"Your road will be long, but I will tell my sisters that you are returned to us."*

"My Lady?"
*"Yes?"*

"Thank you."

## Pantheon

She simply smiled even brighter.

As she kicked into the flanks of her horse
I stood and watched as she sped away
and found my hand returning to
the middle of my chest

There I found the vibration
not to be the resounding thunder of a horse's hooves,
but the beating that I had missed for so long.

# PANTHEON: GRACE

Swarthy and beautiful
She stands amid destruction, clothed in devastation, yet she is
touched by neither
She and I do not meet often, save when frustration's dam has broken
and I am pushed to the brink
In those times when the colors of the world around me are smeared in
the salt ocean swelling in my eyes
As lightly as any angel has ever stepped upon sacred ground, she
moves to me
There is a gentle sway in her hips that causes a flush in my cheeks
when I am fallen in her embrace
She has taught me to bow when the world would have me draw my
sword
Sometimes, she nods knowingly to Mercy and moves so sweetly to
my side, laying slender fingers upon my hand, and with a soft word
douses the fire of my contempt
It is plain unto my own heart, that we are as vastly different as when
her dusky skin is against mine own, in the gentle union of two held
hands
Yet in her sweet form, I see my own
She has never taught me to move to the music of the universe as she
does, yet her devotion is to grant me a communion with it, that I
might appreciate the melody amid the discordant verses of life
And in hearing, so become a servant of her will
Under fire, my mind is still

# **PANTHEON: KARMA**

Get in through the door, finally
Not on the "list" but something tells me she passes the word along
to give me a hard time
Then, up comes the rope and I pass the colossus that guards the
doorway

To this

Her Eden
Playground
Laboratory

Like Odysseus, I follow her siren call
Forgot the wax for my ears
I'll forget so much more before I leave this ancient place

Navigating the sea of humanity that swells and falls between the
notes of the music

A throbbing beat, like her heart
Wild, untamable
Evasive yet, permeating through my blood

Bright spotlights sweep the wave crests of souls that surge back and
forth
Laser-bright beams track across the faces of old and young alike
There are prices for every moment you spend here
The exchange rate is unfair
but exactly what you deserve
She forgives debts
But she demands they be paid

There are things she hates...

Empty promises
Prestidigitation performed with a human heart
Wasted words spreading like spilled ink on a soul's parchment.

I'll find her when she's ready
Fleeting images
Her face hovering over

A slice of flesh, her bare shoulder
Hazel eyes under dark lids, upturned corner of her mouth
A wink under the canopy of her hair, the color of crushed cherries
and bourbon

She'll punish me for searching according to my methods
Raspberry lipstick stains on my heart
in between the bite marks
Currency paid for her affection and time spent in her service

She knows how to play this game
She invented it so long ago
Eventually I will break through the surf of desperation
to find her waiting on the shore

A predator smile on her lips
Glitter at her cheeks…

that I know I will find on my suit
in the morning

She'll advance at my approach
Ever anxious to charge the lightning strike
That she knows is coming…

Pantheon

Fluid motion

as her arms snake around my neck
I'll bow my head to her
The respectful gesture, she insists is not necessary
But the sultry push of her thigh between mine
as she maneuvers her lips to my ear, says otherwise

A gentle bite of my lobe before whispering
*"You're late..."*

Any apology I can muster for keeping her waiting
is quickly snuffed out
by the raging inferno she begins between our mouths
As her teeth sink softly into my bottom lip,
her hand glides deftly to the inside pocket of my jacket
to liberate me of my wallet

Eric Syrdal

# PANTHEON: COURAGE

Sodium light
Cast by one of many tall sentinels
They stand on street corners and along sidewalks
Heads bowed they guard against the night
Throwing their fiery halos onto
the grey landscape of the city

Alone she sits within this circle of protection
Straddles a newspaper dispenser
Just 75 cents gets the latest hysteria of the day
between the folds of black and white ink
Full color fear to reload your magazine
Incentivizing half-cocked knee jerks
for your entertainment

In her hands
between fingers in fingerless gloves
she spins the pommel of a blade
3 feet down on the cement,

its tip leaves a floral design
in white detritus

I recognize its make and model
The scarred edge has seen many battles
Not all of which were victories

Faded T-Shirt
Red sleeves
White body
"42" on the back
Above, in patent vinyl letters
C-RAGE
Jeans that have seen better days
High-topped Converse, ripped at the toe

As I step into her circle
Her deep blue eyes focus on me

Pantheon

Ebony hair

Gathered with a rubber band
and pulled over her left shoulder

With the smile of an old friend
she slides down from her perch,
laying the flat of the sword blade against her shoulder
with the tip pointed at the dark sky above

I am not alone in my entrance to this arena
I hear the footfalls of those that follow me
They stop just outside the circle of light

and offer a collaborative whine

Her cobalt orbs drift from left to right
and back again

"They don't like you being here with me" I offer, knowing that she
understands all too well of whom I speak
I become the source of her attention again.

*"Well that's just too fucking bad, isn't it?"* She says with a wink

Outside the light, I hear whimpering and a low growl

"They've been following me for days."

*"I know."*
"I didn't know I was going to end up here."

She shrugs her shoulders winking, *"Then I would have come looking
for you."* She squints her eyes and peers out into the black
surrounding us. *"How many this time?"*

"I don't know..."

*"Doesn't matter."*

Eric Syrdal


She saunters forward, extending her right hand
As she does, I extend mine too.

When we meet, we clasp each other's forearm
in a warrior's handshake

Around us, my would-be executioners send up a raucous cacophony
of howls

Pealing like discordant church bells, or a calliope being shoved down
a staircase

Feigning to ignore them,
she smiles even brighter and crows-feet show at the sides of her eyes

*"Well met, again, poet."*

"It feels like ages since we were here"
At this, she throws her head back. Her laughter echoes off the
buildings which I know are there but cannot see.
The walls of a silent fortress in the dark of my doubt

*"Like ages? Boy, I'm not sure you know what 'ages' are. As of late, it
is all too frequently I have been called to your side. Not that I don't
adore our time together, but surely there are pursuits in your
universe that do not require my attention so much!"*

I nod, "Of course there are! But perhaps I like our time together as
much as you" I give a casual wink.

A scuffle ensues just outside the light. Vicious snarling accompanied
by a feral roar and a loud shriek, followed by yelping which grows
increasingly softer as its origin moves away

*"They don't like waiting."* she says through her perpetual smile,
*"They'd rather us get on with it."*

"Well who are we to disappoint them?"

*"Before we advance...I want to remind you of someone."*

21

"Who?" I asked.

*"Remember once, long ago, on a chilly morning, a young man straps on armor and prepares for a terrifying adventure?"*

I smile and say, with my tongue planted firmly in my cheek, "I'm sorry I don't recall that."

*"Let me refresh your memory then. His fingers are shaking so badly he can't get the breastplate strap through the buckle..."*

I complete, "so he has to get his best friend to do it for him."

She nods and continues, as she hands me the sword from her shoulder, *"His mouth is dry on the car ride over to the school where she works as a teacher..."*

I fill in, turning to face the darkness beyond our circle of light, "...and he keeps going over the words he will say again and again in his head..."

She picks up where I leave off. I can feel her move behind me, her arms encircling my waist, *"He's not sure he can do this. But it's not for him, it's for her..."*

I close my eyes and lean back against her, gripping the sword tightly in my hand, "There will be a lot of people there..."

I feel her shrug against my back, *"...mostly children..."*

"...and some adults," I continue, "but..."

*"...but he's already there and moving through the crowd to meet her..."*

"She'll be very surprised." I smile.

She chuckles, *"She knows it's coming."*

"But not like this," I continue. "It's morning assembly for the whole school…"

*"…you can see her through the visor of the helm."*

I bark a laugh, "I could barely see anything. My hair got pushed down over my eyes when I put the helmet on…"

She laughs with me, *"You ask the principal to call her down in front…"*

"…and she's so confused. Until…"

She whispers, *"Until you remove the helmet and drop to your knee…"*

"The whole crowd gasped at the same moment. Some people clap, some cheer, mostly the children are giggling."

I feel her rest her forehead against the back of my head, *"But you look up at her and smile…hand her the single rose you brought with you…and pull the ring box from your pocket. Everyone falls silent…"*

"I look at her as she clasps her hand over her mouth, tears starting to fill her eyes."

*"and you said…"*

"I said…"

She and I recite together, "MY LADY? WOULD YOU DO ME THE HONOR OF BECOMING MY WIFE?"

We both fall silent as she moves around in front of me
She holds my face in her hands

and places a tender kiss on my brow

She says, *"Now I ask you…does the man who did all that…have anything…whatsoever…to fear from those mangy mongrels skulking around in the shadows just beyond this halo of light?"*

My eyes embrace hers one last time as I ready myself to charge.
I shake my head in agreement with her

and she offers me one last smile

*"No, of course not. I almost pity them…"* She chuckles, *"…almost"*

Eric Syrdal

# PANTHEON: FATE

Smoke and ash
Popping of cinder and coals
The great hammer falls between her breaths
Sparks like clouds of angry fireflies
erupt and retreat as quickly as they are formed
The cool night air, from the open doorway,
brings relief from the shimmering forge

My passage, seemingly unnoticed by the blacksmith
Deposits me at the threshold of her domain
Walls of wood, floor of earth and straw
Illumination provided by the glow of a super-heated ingot
Masterfully being bent by her will which takes the form of hammer
and anvil

It is as she quenches the rectangular molten form
of a playing card, I find I am not so cleverly unseen

Turning it over in her soot-stained fingers, she lays aside her tools.
She sighs and leans against her workbench
She uses the card to fan the expanse of sun-tanned, sweat-dappled
skin revealed by the open lapels of her shirt.

Her emerald eyes, seemingly lost in thought, track across the room to
my face
They are calm green pools
framed on either side by golden ringlets. Products of the hair piled
high atop her head
and affixed there by a slender rod of iron
The nape of her neck, liberated from her mane, cools in the evening
breeze


My eyes fall upon the card in her hand
This oscillating bringer of relief
Shadowy outline of a single spade in the center
I fail horribly at feigning disinterest

*"I make so few of these lately…"* she smiles. *"When I last forged
your deck you stood no taller than my knee."*

My hand moved to my pocket, feeling the worn and faded pack.
Rectangular pieces of destiny,
held together
by a frayed bit of string and an overstretched rubber band

*"Of course,"* she continued, *"I'm only ever able to place them in
your hands. You have decided to put them up your sleeves and in your
back pocket. And that's when you entered her realm."*

At the exact moment she points to my collar, I reach and smudge my
finger on a stain there
Holding it up to the flickering glow of the forge
Bits of golden flecks of glitter, embedded in rich raspberry lipstick

Seeing my look of embarrassment she laughs, *"Oh blush not for me
warrior heart! I'll wager Karma's exacted her price…but gambling is
not my forte."*

A wry smile and a brief nod from me at the joke whose bill is paid in
full, at my expense

Absentmindedly I pull the deck of cards from my pocket, turning
them over a few times in my hands.

Her eyes light up at the sight of it, *"Ah…of course! You brought them
with you!"*
She stops fanning herself with the ace.

As she approaches me, I take a step back with my left foot.

Primal instinct.
My soul knows her purpose

and of what she is capable.

For one of my blood, her word is final.
Even up to the last moment
when she will speak my name as they lay me in the earth.

Her laughter is surreal.
At once alarming but with the comfort that she is in control and you
are safe in her hands

*"Oh, I often tell the others. I have met no one more respectful than
you, my heart-grounded poet. Your understanding of the work I do
here is remarkable. There is a comfort in knowing that I do not need
to demonstrate with you."*

She stops, very close to me. I find that I am unable to disengage from
her eyes. She holds me there as
a shiver of ice runs down my back

I can smell her sweat mingled with ash from the forge, its fragrance
clings to her and permeates the air between us.

*"Shall we play then?"* As she takes the deck from my trembling hand.
Discarding the ramshackle binding, she thumbs through them one by
one. *"Faro? 5 card stud? Gin rummy? Oh! I know...let's have wild
cards..."*

She is toying with me and taking great pleasure in punishing my
hubris in coming here.

When I offer no reply, she pouts slightly. *"You never have enjoyed
playing with me, have you?"*

She allows me a moment of freedom to slowly shake my head.

*"Smart Boy."*

Holding my deck in one hand, her thumb parts it in two, and in the
gap created there, she files in the newly forged ace

*"A gift"* she says, as she deftly shuffles the cards and then returns the
deck to my pocket. *"A token of my respect for standing on this*

*ground before it is your turn to do so. Bravery is such a flowery word. Let us instead choose to name it...Guile."*

Eric Syrdal

# PANTHEON: MERCY

An angel
Born of neither heaven nor hell…
She stands between the two, existing in this realm of nightmares and
dreams
Not flaxen-haired, nor bright-eyed
A dark child of exquisite beauty, her mane of brown hair, her dark
chestnut eyes
reflecting images of earth

My home

This stage where I am constantly the lead role
Where I go on nightly for the critics
Those souls that inspect my aura
for holes
Gaps in the matrix of my construction

She sits in the front row at each performance
Legs crossed
Hands folded in her lap

When I reach my soliloquy…
The one where I talk about what I have "lost"
And I say that I would rather die than watch my heart turn to stone
And I plunge that dagger through my chest
The popping of the bone in my sternum
The wet *thud* as the blade penetrates my right ventricle…

The blood looks so real…and I have studied, for countless hours, the
human body's reaction to being stabbed so terribly
I am
convincing

Before I fall precisely where the marker is on the stage
so that the trap door opens and I am lowered down in a fog of dry ice
I always look to her face

Because she cries

Pantheon

So softly

Only the gentle flicker of the gas stage lamps catch a glimmer of her
tears
as they drip silently into her lap

I'll admit, there is a wild wave of pride that swells through me
as I understand how intently she watches
So fine an entertainer am I, that I have moved so sweet a creature to
the point of tears
Truly a standing ovation will be in order.

I return at the end of the 3rd act
my death having been a clever ruse
to entrap the ghost of my long dead rival
who has haunted me these long years

He wishes to barter his way into Elysium
using the guise of my soul
to fool Charon into taking him across the river

But it is I who has the final laugh, as I am revealed to be the ferryman
himself!

When we are but halfway across, I capsize the boat.
With my hands about the impostor's throat, I drag him down to the
bottom of the Styx…
Where his soul is ripped apart by the tormented and the damned…

And as my company collects in front of the red curtain
to cheers and applause
amid our bows of thanks
my eyes will search the audience for her beautiful face

But my heart knows I will always find her waiting by the backstage
entrance
A single white rose in her gloved hand
I will greet her, as I have always done
With a bow and a compliment to her great beauty

She will pat her palms together and smile
We will talk of the performance
and she will once again, citing my respect for her, ask me
to *"please stay my hand"* before the destruction of my rival

And I will once again return to her the question:

"If I should rewrite the ending to this play…will it not be my last?

And if it is, on the night of that final performance

will she then remove her gloves and touch my face with her healing
fingers?

And will she, at last, reward me with an escort to the next venue?"

Because if she would agree to my terms…
I'll recall my troupe…
We'll paint our faces and light the stage lamps…
She will be the guest of honor at a private performance…

For I will do ANYTHING…absolutely ANYTHING…to feel her
touch…

And once again, the color will leave her cheeks and with watery eyes
she will say,
*"Not today, Love."*

# **PANTHEON: HOPE CULMINATION**

Salt air and the smell of sand at low-tide
I could hear the waves breaking on the beach
The gentle crashing and then the soft hiss of the
water being drawn back into the ocean again
The wind was out of the north
slightly cooler at the back edge of the front that
had moved through the night before.
Even in the early morning gloaming light,
I could see patches of clouds racing away from me
chasing the storm
Trying to catch up with it like children who missed their school bus

We stood high above the sand
on the breeze swept cliff

As I approached her position
I could feel the reverence of this place
Something in me knew it to be a place of
great sacrifice

*"It's still a couple of hours away…"* she said, turning her head
slightly to speak over her shoulder. *"It was supposed to happen
yesterday…Did you know that?"*

Of course I did…I knew where we were…I've spent years of my life
learning about this place
I nodded, then felt like an idiot because she wasn't looking at me.

*"Of course you do…"* she spoke to my unseen nodding *"I always
believed that when Karma decided it was going to happen…Fate
threw that storm-front in,"* she gestured over her shoulder, *"just to
fuck with everyone. She doesn't like being told what to do."*

"Well," I said, "the world is on fire…and someone has to put it out."

As I got closer
I slowed my pace, breathing in the sight of her

Her hair flowed down from victory rolls on either side
It spilled down her back in golden rapids and lay loose about her
shoulders
A few strands tangled in the medals at her left breast
The olive drab coat, cinched tight at the waist by a thick, wide,
leather belt
On her right hip, a holster and a service revolver
A skirt, covered her legs to the knee

My eyes followed her
powerful calves, down to her elegant feet, tucked neatly into patent
leather shoes
Everything with a surface that could shine, did.

Cobalt blue eyes watched me
above raspberry colored lips that parted only slightly
But gave no hint of any welcoming smile…

Eager to break the silence, I spoke first, "This is not where I expected
to find you."

*"Why?"* she said, resting a hand on her hip.

I shrugged. I honestly didn't know why.
I started to attempt an answer but she beat me to it, *"Is there no better
place than this for me to exist?"*
She was right. There was no better place than this for her to exist.

Seeing an unwillingness from me to answer her question, she
continued

*"Those men out there in the dark. They are getting ready to converge
here and they expect to find me waiting."*

She turned her head to look over her shoulder, out into the dark
horizon.
*"They are getting onboard all manner of floating deathtraps to come
to this place. They're being packed like sardines into landing craft,
with nothing more than the equipment they were given this
morning…and the hands that Fate has dealt them."*

Subconsciously I put my hand in my pocket and felt the deck of cards there.

*"But not all of those hands include aces,"* she gave me a sidelong glance, *"Newly forged or otherwise. Some of them are just complete crap."* she takes a deep sigh, *"Most of them are crap."*

She sees my uncomfortable fidgeting. But she continues anyway

*"Right now, Courage is going around and telling stories to them. Reminding them of the times they have saved lives…or the times where they have made a difference…just a time or two when they were brave. Of course, there can be no bravery without fear. You know that? Don't you?"*

"Yes." I answer, "It's not the absence of fear. It's acting in spite of it."

*"Not your words, poet?"*

"No Ma'am." I answer, "But they are good words."

*"Your Grandfather is out there right now…and your Great Uncle. They don't know what hand has been dealt to them, yet."* she points to my feet, *"But you do. Because you are standing in front of me now."*
*"So they're afraid. But she's talking to them the same as she talks to you. And whatever story she digs up down from deep in their mind it obviously works."*

She smiles, *"We can take comfort in that. So I ask you, could any of them do what will need to be done, in the next few hours, if they thought I wouldn't be here? When they have traveled so far and sacrificed so much to get here?"*

"No." I answer

*"Of course not."* she nods, *"Nor could they accept the fact that many of them will never see home again. When they fall overboard into the bloody surf, Grace will do her best to get them back to their feet. But,*

*it may very well be Mercy's hand they need to take in order to leave this terrible day behind them."*

She leaves a long, uncomfortable silence for a while. Then moving forward she extends her hand and I take it.

*"You say, sometimes, that you cannot see me? You know how I wither away when all you do is let fear, doubt, anger, hate, and desire take up residence in your soul. I know how far you wander away from us, and how you hate yourself for doing so."* she squeezes my hand tightly, *"But each time you come back to us, you restore my hope in you and you let me live with you, again."*

We stand there, holding hands…listening to the surf and the wind…

She whispers, but I hear it as if she were raising her voice above all the loudest sounds in the world.

*"There's a reason that I am found on battlefields everywhere. Because I am necessary to do the things that must be done and the deeds that exact the hardest payment. Because I offer the promise that it was not all done in vain. And I bring the knowledge that it is worth the effort to grab onto that promise and hold on."*

She lifts my hand in hers and holds it in front of my face… *"You can always hold on to me, poet. Remember that."*

# WARSONG

Eric Syrdal

## WARSONG
## Systolic

The morning is still
The colors of the new dawn stretch over the horizon
Long fingers of pink, orange, violet
The arms of the sun stretching out to push back the blanket
of night.
The last buzzing and chattering of night insects
fade away in the tall grasses
Assembled on this hillside
we gather to the clarion call of her banner

The blood-red and gold threads in the fabric
shimmer as it waves and flutters
Despite the lack of wind, held aloft by will
The will of those that travel to it

Those who get up upon their ragged legs
With sore backs and broken hearts
they bring their weapons
Some light and sharp tucked into scabbards of gold
Some dull and heavy, heaved upon shoulders or dragged in the mud
I await my turn at the roster

Stepping to the podium, I look upon the ledger and find my name

Skald, Wordsmith

Laying my arms at my feet
I dip both hands into the fount next to The Great Book
Filling them with the Water of Life, I bathe my face

As I allow the water to drip from my chin
I close my eyes and breathe in the morning air
My feet feel strong upon this ground
When the sun finally rises over those mountains
I will stand at the ready
To receive my blessings before battle
As I make my way back to the center

39

of this martial assembly
I am path-crossed by a familiar face

Hope drifts past me like a vision

She has the cobalt eyes, but not the ebony hair
Of her more warrior-esque sister

She has the golden hair of finality
She has the bright smile of chance
She has the stance of fluidity
She has the lilt in her voice of universal harmony
She has exchanged her dress uniform for a white toga
glittering gold laurels shine in her hair
and on her feet, are deep brown sandals that form an intricate network
of knotted straps
up her legs

We exchange a nod of acknowledgement as she floats by like a cloud
I expected to have a dialogue, but she taps her finger to her lips
and I hear her voice in my head

*"Remember that which Fate has given you, dear poet. Remember that
they are not quite so powerful when you use them...as when they are
used for someone else."*

I nod my head as our eyes say goodbye

She disappears into the assembly and I notice that she draws the
attention of no one else

A rough shove at my back
brings me back to the now
as I spin to look, my heart flutters like a butterfly in a cage

Those same cobalt orbs I just left have returned to embrace me
belonging to a warrioress of great power

There is a clap of a thunderbolt as we clasp hands
Surging power of the ocean in her grip

Her midnight hair is bound in two thick braids that relax against her
breastplate
Her powerful form is hidden beneath her armor
But her calming smile still stands prominently enough on her
beautiful face

What man could not conquer any battle when Courage stands beside
him?

*"Oh, the enemy is going to be pissed today!"* No echo for her
laughter this time, but my ears love the sound of it all the same.

"I have to admit, seeing you here has made me feel a lot better,
already."

*"Where the hell else would I be, boy?"* she cranes her neck to look
over my shoulder, *"Have you seen her yet?"*

"Who?" I ask like an idiot

Her head still looks over my shoulder but those eyes drift back with
raised brows, *"You messing with me?"*

I raise both my hands in front of me, palms out, in mock surrender,
"nope."

*"Usually she's here by now. I wonder what's keeping her? No big
deal, we won't miss the commotion when she gets here."* she looks
around the assembly, *"Quite a crowd, huh?"*

I nod, "Yep…who are all these people?"

*"You,"* she responds, *"Well, not exactly. They are pieces of you….but
entities unto themselves. It's complicated, to explain…."*

I look to the face of a man standing nyearby.
Nondescript clothes, baggy grey and brown.
Muted colors
A few ruddy leather plates strapped to hands and legs, something like

quilted armor over his chest

His face is weathered, probably from a lifetime in the fields
His arms are tough but he sags in the middle, and he seems to favor
his right leg
A dusting of brown stubble at his cheeks and his hair is cropped clean
to his scalp.
A woven cap of dull green sits slightly to the back of his head,
covering the tops of his ears
there is a scar on his left cheek, just below his eye
But something in the eyes…for a brief moment we engage each other
in a glance
I get the feeling I'm looking at a long-lost friend whose name I can't
quite place
My stomach crawls around little in my gut, and I take a deep breath

"What happens when they…" I can't finish the sentence

But she does, *"Die?"*

"Uh….yeah…" I can feel the color draining out of my cheeks

She shrugs, *"I don't know to tell you the truth. If it's not too many,
probably nothing."*

"Probably?" I retort

She shakes her head, *"Don't worry about it. We're gonna do fine
today"*

I nod a few times as we seem to have run out of things to talk about.
The prospect of losing "pieces of me" to whatever is going to happen
here has kind of killed the mood.

I'm relieved when she decides to speak again, *"Besides,"* she points
and I look to where she indicates. *"If she's here, I'll wager that we've
nothing to really worry about."*

Higher up the hill I see a woman of burly build, picking her way
through the crowded mass of people.
She's headed for the podium.

Her unkept blond hair piled up atop her head
She carries a massive hammer in her right hand as she strides forward

Upon reaching The Great Book, she lays her hammer to rest and
begins thumbing through
the pages

Her emerald eyes scan the names one by one
and she mouths them in turn, no sound escaping her lips
At first, I find it quite odd
Then, an ice-cold shiver runs down my spine
as a realization hits me

When she speaks a name
things happen
The ice-cold shiver transforms to frozen fire
as she stops reading and I understand her green eyes
are fixed on me
*"You seem determined to stand on ground that is awfully close to
me."*

Unnerving though they are, her eyes deliver other emotions
Like the feeling that her presence means you are absolved of
decisions
Blame and consequence are lifted
if only for a short while

*"I think because I have a tendency to smile, when we speak, you are
encouraged to approach me as if you are in the presence of an old
friend. Believe me when I tell you, you could not be more wrong. It is
a dangerous proposition to believe me so fond of you that you are
perfectly safe on this field. "*

The unconscious reaction of my left foot taking a step back brings a
chuckle to her lips.

*"That's better."*

I stand there as her eyes drift back to the pages
The seconds move by so slowly here
and I know everything takes place between a single heartbeat and the
next
I am thankful that she doesn't look at me when she speaks again,

*"You are feeling relieved because you see me here, poet. Because you
believe that having Fate on your side means victory."* she closes the
book and picks up her hammer resting it on her shoulder, *"Nothing
can be further from the truth. Because I do not choose sides."*

She smiles as she steps from the podium and heads back up the
hillside to her tent.

*"If I were you, I'd keep my guard up."*

Eric Syrdal

## WARSONG
## Deconstruction of Fear

Thunder
But no lightning strike before hand
It rumbles across the sky behind me

As I watch the golden haired architect
of my future stride away from me
I can feel the reverberation of the rumbling through
my boots
My mind begins to decipher the vibrations
and determine their true origin
Hoof-beats
I turn…and am greeted with a heroic sight

On the back of her massive ebony war steed
The Queen approaches

The morning sun crests the peaks of the eastern mountains
as it falls across her armor, she is lit up like a scarlet flame
atop a massive piece of lumbering coal
with the power of a freight train the beast surges forward
The mass of souls that have gathered here part like water
before her advance.

Behind her
Her attendants file in line, crimson banners flap in the
wake of their passing. The tinkling of their barding mixes with
the earthquake of their arrival, sounding more like a temple sundering
to the ground, the closer they get to my position.

As they pass my fellow soldiers, men and women alike drop to their
knees and bow their heads
I will hold my gaze upon her
until she reaches such a distance
that my knee will fall to earth like a lodestone to a steel plate
I shall absolutely bow my head to her
To avoid having to look into the ice-blue of her eyes

Pantheon

But time and history, recorded in white scars, show I will make
contact with them at some point

She'll rein in my fire
and mold it to her efforts
I laugh a little to myself
then I notice the thunder is gone
and I feel the presence of someone looking at me
I wait for centuries before I take a deep breath
and then my fears are confirmed as she speaks
into the morning air

*"Arise, Poet."*

I rise to my feet, planting them squarely on either side of me.
I lower my shield and keep my hand clear of my weapon

Her flowing amber hair has been tucked back into a tight braid
snaking out from the back of her head
It falls across one shoulder and lays there like the dark orange tail of a
dragon
Her helm, fashioned into the likeness of a crown, casts a small
window of gold
on the ground in front of me
The raised visor reveals those same ice-blue eyes
But her freckles are gone today
and her lips are flushed a deep crimson

As she dismounts
the rest of her entourage does as well
For a brief moment the clamor of creaking leather and armor
is deafening,
She hands the reins of her steed to her nearest adjutant
and moves quickly to my position
Since she bid me to stand, I'd been focusing on a point on the
horizon, just over
her left shoulder
But honestly what was the point?

*"You still think not looking at me is going to keep you out of our conversation?"*

"No, Your Majesty."

She does sour looks very well
I am almost sorry
I know she hates that.

*"Very well…"* she keeps the tone in her voice even, *"Let's walk and you can look at the ground while we talk. So you don't trip and fall."*

I bow slightly, holding my hand out to the side
gesturing for her to lead the way

*"I think we'll walk side by side for this chat, if you please?"*

"Of course, My Lady. Whatever you wish."

As she moves in beside me, I measure my steps.
Not too fast.
I see we are proceeding towards the front line
and I'd like to delay that trip as long as possible
I admit, she was taking her time getting the conversation started
I half thought she had decided to mock me by not saying
a word until I looked her in the eye
To my displeasure, I was wrong…

*"You are not a coward, poet."*

Unsure of how to answer this, I pursed my lips and shook my head.
"Not to my
knowledge, My Lady…No…"

*"It was a statement, not a question."*

"AH! Then I agree with you."

*"Then why do you pretend to be?"*

Where was she going with this?
"I'm really not sure wha-"

*"You don't know what I mean?"*

"No, My Lady"

*"Why do you choose to give the impression that you want nothing to do with conflict?"*

"I've always believed that in order to live a healthy life, one should avoid conflict whenever possible."

She stops and I do too...thankful for the pause in our trip.
She points to the quill pen sticking out of my back pocket, *"Yet when you search my memories and write them down with that pen you show time and time again that conflict is part of life."*

She had me there, "Yes, but-"

*"But conflict doesn't have to happen if you avoid it. Does it? You can hide from it until it quietly passes you by like a blind beast looking elsewhere for its supper?"*

I take a deep breath, "No, it doesn't"

*"So why do you hide from it?"*

Of course I know the answer she wants to hear, "Fear."

She continues to walk and I follow beside her again

*"You see? You use THAT word like you believe in it. Like it governs part of your life. Yet you don't do you?"*

"I don't what?"

*"Believe in it. You don't believe that fear rules you. After all what is it?"*

"Anxiety about what might happen."

She nods her head, *"What might happen as a result of..."*

"Failure..." I finish.

*"Whose failure?"* she prods

I suck in a breath of air over my teeth, "You know whose."

*"I do indeed. But, if we are to come to an understanding you must say it. If we are to be triumphant on this field, you must acknowledge why we are here..."*

"Fine. Mine."

*"...and how do you believe you will fail?"*

"Not being where I am supposed to be, when I am supposed to be. Following a dead-end street for so long, that to backtrack to the main road means years wasted! Never remembering my dreams...only my nightmares....Not being there for others...when they most needed me...and they're lost forever...BEING A POET AND FOLLOWING MY HEART WHEN I SHOULD FOLLOW MY HEAD.." I hadn't noticed the rising contempt in my voice.
I immediately regretted it.

I come to a stop, because in my periphery I notice she is no longer walking beside me.
Turning around I see her standing several paces behind.
I backtrack my steps until I am standing in front of her again.
I wanted to apologize. Why must she push me to these confessions?

She speaks
I expect to hear anger in her voice. But, of course, there is none

*"You believe that if you take on the responsibility of things that are not your fault, Fate will spare you future grief. Because you think she keeps score and that she is moved by your charity and selfless nature. We all wish she was...she is not...she does not keep score. She is*

*indiscriminate in her distribution of pain and parsimonious when it comes to her distribution of joy."*

I no longer had a problem resisting the urge to look at her. Right now the ground was a much better subject.

*"But there is one of us that does keep score. She watches you just as intently as Fate ever has. She deciphers your intentions behind your actions…and she does look favorably on the burdens you choose to carry. I have never known a time when she was unhappy to see you…as often you have had her raspberry lipstick somewhere on your face. And she will be watching today as well…."* she sighs, *"This is where I leave you, for now…"*

I shake my head, "So you will not ride into battle with me today?"

*"Of course I will! When it is time…"* she says, as I hear her walking forward.

She has removed her gauntlet and extends a hand to rest upon my shoulder. As I drop to my knee I look up into her face at last…

*"Do you remember Tennyson?"* she asks, her eyes searching my face

"Yes. Ulysses."

*"The lines which bring tears to your eyes?"*

"Of course."

*"Remember **that which you are**, poet."*

"I will, My Lady."

*"Amor Vincit Omnia"*

I close my eyes briefly as I feel her hand retract.
I listen to the soft shuffling of her feet as she moves away from me in the dew-soaked grass.

Here is where the line will form.
I am the center
I will not break

## WARSONG
## Diastolic

As I look to my left and right
the battle line runs in each direction
to the horizon
A gentle breeze blows across the valley before us
It picks up our standards
They pop and flutter above our heads
Bright sunlight
Scattering colors across the assembled troops
grey, silver, iron
chain and cloth
canvas

Wool, dyed in vibrant colors of homelands far away
sword frogs, rattling with brass and copper scabbards
Family heirloom jewels twinkle on hilts and cross guards
Horse hair tufts, or beautiful plumage of exotic birds wave
from the tops of helms
Shields, emblazoned with family crests
mottos in Latin
pledging fealty or declaring independence

The ground is solid beneath my feet
My shield is heavy, as always, but my arm feels strong
My grip on the hilt of my sword is firm
I'm gripping it so tightly I feel like I might leave the
impression of my fingerprints in the leather wrapping

Behind our line, further up the hill
The Queen sits on her steed
The main battle standard in the grip of her right hand
Her entourage flanks her on either side
Small company of archers in front
and behind a shield-wall
of footman
A well armored smattering of red and black on the green
of the hillside

Off to my right I hear a familiar voice

*"Are you sure you remember what I taught you to do with that thing?"*

I don't need to look to see who it is, but I do anyway
Ebony hair, deep blue eyes, mischievous smile

"I think I'm holding it right, at least?"

I love her laughter

*"Yeah, I think so…"*

She breaks ranks and moves to my side
reaching over she squeezes my upper arm

*"Not much we can do about this, I'm afraid."*

I shrug with a smile, "Not really…maybe I should be discharged?"

*"Not a chance,"* she pats my arm…and it actually hurts a little, *"Not today at least."*

"I'm scared." I admit

*"Why do you think I'm standing here?"*

I chortle, "yeah, I know…"

*"Relax… just remember everything I've taught you. Play your cards right… You're going to be fine."*

"What's out there? What are we up against?"

She closes her eyes for a few moments, just standing there.
There is an eerie silence here. I had expected a battlefield to be more raucous.
But as I wait for her answer…I feel like I am present at a
funeral…right before someone is about to deliver the eulogy.

Pantheon

*"Primordial Fear…The thing under your bed…nights spent staring at the curtains in your room until you could make out the pale light of dawn…broken hearts…lost toys…rejection…misunderstood good intentions…soul staining lies… disappointment… unreachable goals… failed attempts… truths about yourself that you hate… pain… both emotional and physical… the failures of your body in its older age… catastrophe… devastation… loneliness… a lifetime of memories snuffed out in the wake of a storm"*

I could hear the sound of my own breathing in my ears, a fluttering in my gut…like liquid having been stirred in a cauldron…slowly churning…

*"But there is also Hope."*

My eyes had drifted away from her face while she was naming all the terrible things we would find…when they returned I could feel the worry leaving my limbs… swept away by her smile.

*"She's out there isn't she?"*

*"Every time"*

I take a wide survey of the valley.  The sky has been mostly clear all morning, but a few clouds have rolled in. Their shadows drift across the features of the ground below us. Rock outcroppings…a shallow river tumbling over smooth stones…patches of pink and yellow wildflowers.

Such a beautiful place to be destroyed so utterly between the collapsing walls of two armies.
On the far side…on the ridge directly opposite us… something was beginning to take form

At first, I dismissed it as the gathering shadows of clouds

My eyes were starting to pick out shapes over there now…
The distance played tricks with discerning size and number
But it was clear that whatever was over there was strong in force

like a wall of shadow…it undulated and grew
staining the grass like pitch
easily stretching out across the horizon
A threatening horde of the unspeakable
it began to form a clear line

Tattered and shredded battle standards took flight
as the wind began to blow out of the north
A low moaning drifted to my ears
Like a monastic chant…deep pitched and guttural
Interspersed with a wailing
Primal sorrow
Keening at the dark sky at midnight
calling things from the deepest parts of hell
and something else

Something "unnameable"
Unreal
It was massive, gargantuan
It moved behind their battle-line
Horn tipped, winged, scaled
As it paced back and forth like a wounded animal in a cage
the other parts of the gathering host
shrank and moved away from its presence
like shadows falling away from light
Whatever it was
It knew me
and I
it

"So how do we start this?"  I asked, drawing my sword from its
scabbard

Around me, the same motion was repeated for every soldier within
sight.
Weapons were drawn from sheaths brought to the ready beside
shields.
The sheer force of the unified movement stalled my breath for a
second

*"We'll move on your command."* she said, and readied her own
weapon

As if defining exactly what she meant I took a step forward with my
right foot
and the entire battle line, from each horizon to my position…did
exactly the same

A thunder-clap of noise, as each soldier stepped at the same time
When I followed with my left
the ensuing echo took minutes to dissipate

I raised an eyebrow and smiled at her
She returned it with a wide, white-toothed grin of her own

I raised my sword over my right shoulder
and with all the strength I could muster
I shouted the order at the top of my lungs

"CHARGE!"
It's an impressive sight to see.
Even more to be a part of.
A unified, heavily armored, massive entity
made up of brave souls bristling with defiance
in the face of terror
We poured down the hillside
Passion and gravity making each stride carry us
yards at a time
with superhuman speed

Ahead of us
the legions of our foe rained down the opposite side
of the valley
A black cascade of crude oil and soot
gangling, malformed limbs

Ragged faces, slobbering tongues and teeth
Fangs and claws
Poison spines and cloven hooves

I brought my shield to the ready,
tucked my head behind the guard and prepared for the impact of first contact
I was not prepared for what met me, however…

Bone-jarring force
picked me up like a child's toy and flung me through the air
I crashed to the ground 10 to 15 feet away from the collision
I lay, flat on my back, looking skyward

As I struggled to refill my lungs with precious oxygen
I could feel the weight of my shield at my throat
The iron edge digging into my skin
I was no longer holding my sword
It had been blasted from my grip

I felt around me, confirming that my arm was not broken at least,
Stretching out wide above my head
my fingers touched the hilt and I managed to curl my hand around the pommel
Dragging it to my side, I began to try to sit up
I closed my eyes tightly against the fireworks exploding behind them
My mouth parted and I gulped down a throat-full of air
I convulsed with a cough
My stomach heaved as my head swirled
Using the tip of my blade as a crutch, I first got to my knees
Then began working my way to my feet
My trajectory had thrown me clear of the fighting
The swirling melee was at least 20 to 30 feet away from me moving forward
As my breath tried to stabilize, I began to hobble back towards the line

I approached and the enemy began to take notice of my return
A few of the dark shadows began to peel off from the fighting

Two slender forms, almost reptilian in shape
began to stalk towards me, hissing, snapping teeth
I focused my attention on the lead
bringing my sword and my shield to bear

Its first attack bangs noisily off my shield
As it tries for a second strike, I bring an overhead chop that
bites deep into its neck

I hear the second attacker strike from the rear and I tense my
muscles to receive the blow
But nothing happens

Then I feel a pressure at my back
Someone standing against me
My lips part, a broad smile in the midst of war
as I hear from behind me,

*"First you take a nap?... then you decide that your first engagement
in this fight is with TWO targets? I like your ambition, Boy, but I
think you should take a little time to get familiar... don't you think? I
think you overestimate those cards in your pocket..."*

I open my mouth to answer but she cuts me off

*"MOVE RIGHT!"*

I slide my feet over and pivot on my right foot. A shadow that was
advancing on my flank is met by my blade.
I cut it down with three hard blows, wrenching my weapon free of its
dying corpse.

As I recover, she speaks again.

*"LEFT SIDE!  SHIELD!"*

I bring my aegis up and receive a shattering blow that shoves the edge
into my left temple. More fireworks of pain...but thanks to her
warning, I'm still alive...

As I try to recover, I swing my blade wide in an arc that severs a limb
of my attacker
it flops to the earth and convulses there while its owner turns,
screeching and snarling

It bolts from me and I plant both feet firmly before propelling myself
after it.

I chase it for a short distance until it is cornered near a rock
outcropping.
Turning, it cradles its ruined arm with its other…arches its back and
lowers its vulpine head and distends its jaw in a freakishly wide gape.

Confidently I square my stance, raising my blade to advance in.
It moves forward and as I brace for a charge, it darts with lightning
speed

Directly around me
and disappears into the swirling battle several feet away

As I turn to watch it flee…
Something in my stomach feels like an ice-cold hand has reached
inside me and clenched my gut

I open my mouth to try to suck in air…but my lungs won't fill
I raise a hand to my throat…as if I can squeeze the air down into my
chest
My vision blurs and white flashes begin to flicker in my periphery
before I know it, I have collapsed to my knees
I release my sword and my shield
they tumble from my grasp and fall to the ground

The land around me has turned from green grass to oil soaked mud
I can feel my knees sinking in it
My hands are clawing at my throat now…trying to clear whatever is
blocking my airway
A searing fire begins in my chest
Panic is flooding behind my eyes
I am crippled and paralyzed…

I know it is only a matter of time before one of the shadows sees me
as a defenseless target and ends this
But no attack has come

Pantheon

I feel the cold presence of something behind me
Turning slowly, my knees hampered by the mud
I finally come face to face with it
It towers over me
Its skin crawls, rippling patterns of scales
Almost alive and with a mind of its own
Powerful wings adorn its shoulders
They are drawn down across its back
Its ragged maw hangs open with a jaw like a giant
Steel bear trap
Razor-sharp fangs form a wall of swords across its
face
I can feel its tepid breath, watching as its chest rises and falls
emitting a low growl

Massive sharp talons support its weight and sink down into the mud
as it takes a few steps to balance its enormous bulk
Two eyes, like molten iron, glare out from a horned brow
I was not prepared for the roar that came from its gut
Like a soul being dragged down to hell
A wailing, so loud and fierce, I felt my ears might begin to bleed

Gone was the sunlight and the blue sky
An eerie dark haze formed around this meeting
I held my arms out behind me as I fell backward

They did little to stop my descent
My palms slick with blood and sweat
Slid quickly on the surface of the mud
Bringing my head down to the ground with a crash
I then managed to draw in one sickly breath as I pushed hard
with my feet and shoved myself away from this horror
propelling myself backward as quickly as I might
to slam into the surface of the rock

Cornered prey
Ripe for the taking
The monstrosity began a slow crawl forward
Sniffing the air wildly

Never ceasing its growling
Enjoying the flavor of my panic
It seemed to be taking its time, moving almost in slow motion

Suddenly…I was no longer alone….

She slid in next to me
She had abandoned her weapons
I could see her face
She was talking to me
But my ears weren't hearing anything

Her cobalt blue eyes stayed locked on mine
Her expression was reassuring….
She was pointing to my pocket
and gesturing wildly
She wanted me to get something from there
Asking me something
No
Begging me to do something
I stood by and watched as my hand felt down inside
and pulled out an object
brown, rectangular
She nodded and took it from me
Everything swam back into focus

*"…Ok? I'm sorry I let you get away from me. We're going to get you out of here…you're going to be fine. OK?"*

She began thumbing through the playing cards like a madwoman.

*"No….no…….no…..come on…it's got to be here"*

I was confused…what was she looking for?
I watched her hands…so delicate and powerful at the same time.
She got to the end of the deck and began rifling through it again.

*"SONOFABITCH!! COME ON!! It's in here. I know she gave you one!!!"*

Pantheon

I watched card after card go by in her fingers

…face cards…clubs…diamonds…hearts…spades…

I think it was the 3 of diamonds that I saw last when she was struck

A massive talon swung in between us.
The claw caught just under her breast-plate
I saw it pierce straight through, warm blood exploded in my face
I just stared at her
The confused expression on her face
Eyebrows wrinkled in question
as she rocketed away from me
And a trail of playing cards fluttered out in her wake as she flew,
like oversized confetti

She landed hard
Lifeless, no movement

My head snapped to the origin of the blow
The massive thing had turned and was following the fluttering cloud
of cards
as they drifted on the winds of war eventually making their way to the
ground
It had lost interest in me for the moment

I focused on her body

No, she was not moving
Her head was turned away from me

I got to my hands and knees
darting my eyes between the beast and
my destination. I began to crawl
like an infant
My hands sunk into the mud
The foul stench of blood and sweat wafted up with each crawling step
it gagged me and made me cough

Eric Syrdal

I pushed hard
clawing and scraping my way across the ground

I had to reach her
I had to
I kept trying to focus my ears
on the sounds behind me
Hoping that the thing was still occupied with the scattered cards
But my mind killed all extraneous thought
as soon as I reached her

I pulled myself up and across her body

The jagged pieces of her broken armor cut through my t-shirt
I was certain I was gouging deep holes in my chest
But I didn't care

I wiped the mud, as completely as I could, from my hands
very gingerly took both sides of her head and rotated her face
around to look at me

The sludge had matted her hair to her forehead
A thick slurry of blood was dripping from the side
of her mouth
Her eyes focused on mine
I saw the muscles in her cheeks try to pull her face
into a smile
But it did not work

Her eyes welled with tears
as did mine
She closed her eyes hard and moved her mouth
Forming her lips
but no air could escape from her collapsed lungs
I understood well enough

"It's ok," I said

She opened her eyes and kept them locked on mine
Even as I lowered my forehead to hers

Pantheon

I held her gaze as long as I could before the tears forced me to close
my eyes
When I opened them again, hers were closed

An agonizing howl escaped my lips
I laid her head back gently on the ground and laid my head against
her breastplate
sobbing like a child

A roar brought my situation back into focus
As I looked up
the massive thing had lost interest in the scattered cards
It was making its way back over to me
with glowing eyes and teeth bared

A volcanic eruption began to build inside me and I drew in a deep
breath

As I stood up, I looked down at her body one last time

Something caught my attention in her right gauntlet
Something peeking out from her fingers
I reached down and opened her palm
The face on a playing card stared back at me

The Queen of Hearts

Plucking it from her palm
I held it tightly in my hands
Then refocusing on the lumbering behemoth making its way towards
me
I crouched down and laid it on the ground between us

Several seconds passed before I noticed it vibrating
then it began to flop around the ground like a landed fish on a river
bank
and I began to understand why
I could feel the thunder through my legs
rising up through my spine

Eric Syrdal

Something told me to remain low to the ground

and I did

A massive black shadow, ridden by a crimson flame burst from the
darkness behind me
and sailed through the air over my head

The impact was spectacular
A freight train bursting through a glass warehouse
2000 pounds of draft horse and armored warrior
The creature met with a horrific collision
bones and muscle being broken and torn
leather wings crumpling under the blow
it turned end over end to rest finally more than 100 feet away

I turned,
Sure that my flank was completely protected
I knelt down and pulled Courage into my lap

I'm not a strong man
but I cradled her armored body in my arms

After a few seconds I was able to get my
knees to stop wobbling and shaking
I stood and made my way over to meet
my rescuer

I made no attempt to look away from her
in this moment she was more beautiful than she ever could have been
She pulled hard on the reins and looked down at me

*"Come with me now, poet! That beast is only stunned. It would take a
lot more than that to kill it."*

She had a confused look on her face as she looked from Courage to
me and back

*"Leave her here! We need to fall back."*

Pantheon

"No"

*"Poet, we have no time for this. We need to regroup."*

"... take her..." a whispered plea

She sighs a sigh so full of pain and she looks away from me
*"There is nothing you can do for her now"*

"Please, My Lady. You have to take her..."

*"No, I need to take YOU....We'll order a retreat and regroup at the
camp. It will be nightfall soon. Under cover of darkness we'll think
this through and come up with another strategy. We'll rally and
attack in the morning"*

Spend the night thinking this over
mulling it through
what could be done differently
what could be done to prevent this
wondering
agonizing, until dawn brings the morning light
to stinging, bloodshot eyes
No,
no more sleepless nights over this
no more
I had to do this for me
For Courage at least
I owed her that much

She noticed I was no longer looking at her.
Just staring down at the body in my arms.
The Queen's voice moves to a whisper, but I am always able to hear
it

*"Listen to me, Love. You have to leave her here..."*

"I CAN'T!!!" The shout echoes like it's inside a small room, I
swallow hard and my voice cracks."I can't leave her here"

She urges her mount forward until she is right next to me.
She leans down, and with one arm, she takes Courage's lifeless form
and hauls it over the front of her saddle. It's like laying a child's rag-
doll across a bench
I step back and nod a few times….trying to take deep breaths…
failing…

*"What will you do? You have no more cards…If you come back with
me now… I might be able to convince Fate to-"*

"They're not all gone."

She is puzzled and her horse takes a nervous step backward as the
beast begins to stir

"Please, My Lady. Go back." My voice is full of steel and conviction
"I'll be fine. I know what I have to do."

I wait to argue
I know she is going to push me
to go back with her
She is going to command it
And I'll run with her

I'll run away and leave this battle to be fought again and again
night after bloody night

So when she moves past me
And I look up and see her watching me over her shoulder
as her horse picks its way between the devastation on the hillside….

I raise my hand in farewell
and move it to my own heart
and watch her as long as I can
Until the maelstrom around me comes flooding back into focus
Behind me, the beast is trying to prepare for another attack

I hear the popping of its broken bones as it forces its way up onto its
feet

Pantheon

Its wings are ripped and hang down from its sides like rags
but its horrible face is firmly targeted on my position
and it begins to hobble and limp forward
its ruined back leg is making it difficult

Nearby I see my sword and shield lying in the mud
between my challenger and myself
I take a step forward
Here I am again
alone
on this battlefield
This ancient foe waiting to slake its thirst on my blood
It's time to stop running from this
Time to stop hiding
Verses from Tennyson's "Ulysses" come flooding into my heart...
My lips begin moving as the words form in my mind...

**"Tis not too late to seek a newer world.**
**Push off, and sitting well in order smite**
**The sounding furrows; for my purpose holds**
**To sail beyond the sunset, and the baths**
**Of all the western stars, until I die..."**

I reach my shield...and reaching down with one hand, I pluck it from
the mud
bringing it to my left arm, I fasten the buckle there, pulling it tight
and into position.

**"It may be that the gulfs will wash us down:**
**It may be we shall touch the Happy Isles,**
**And see the great Achilles, whom we knew..."**

As I reach my sword, I pick it up.
The pommel feels like a feather in my hand.
I slide it securely into its scabbard.
And then with my free, right hand, I reach around to my hip pocket.
My fingers grasp an object there
closing over its smooth surface

**"Tho' much is taken, much abides; and tho'**

Eric Syrdal

**We are not now that strength which in old days**
**Moved earth and heaven, that which we are, we are..."**

The beast surges forward
desperately trying to close the distance
Its maw dripping with hate and contempt for me
Its eyes focus on the object I bring around in front of me
and raise within the field of its vision

**"One equal temper of heroic hearts. . ."**

The words Hope said to me before the battle drive my actions now

*"Remember that they are not quite so powerful when you use*
*them...as when they are used for someone else..."*

I could use this
and make all of this go away
I could use this
and make my own path clear of obstacles
I could use this
and no one would be the wiser
Or
I could use this

in the name of peace
in the name of persistence
in the name of right
with the courage to do what I must
I could do this for her

I hold the ace of spades between my thumb and forefinger...

The beast roars
it sounds painful this time
more like a howl of agony
I reach forward and take the opposite corner of the card between the
fingers of my other hand

**"Made weak by time and fate, but strong in will. . ."**

Pantheon

It's more than desperate now
It lunges forward
Mud flying as it tries to reach me

Its jaws now just a few yards from my position

**"To strive. . ."**

Now just a few feet.....

**"to seek. . ."**

I begin to tear the playing card in half
to sacrifice the easy path
and begin a journey on the hardest road I have ever known
A white light emanates from the rip
bathing both the creature and Me in a glow
The glow of the beginning of the universe
anything that has been or will be

**"to find. . ."**

The hot fetid breath of the snapping jaws are inches away now…
and in one last, panicked effort it lunges for the kill…

**"and not to yield…"**

As I speak the final words of Tennyson's Poem
I tear the card in half. . .

There is a blinding flash
and the last image I recall seeing is
the creature, erupting in white flames and disintegrating into
nothingness

Then all is black

I am awakened to weighted silence
Flat on my back

The sky has turned
to the soft pink and orange of sunset

I see her face hover over me
Grace extends a slender-fingered
dark-skinned hand
and with the strength of a titan
she pulls me to my feet
My shield lies shattered
sundered and broken
kindling and splinters
As I smile at Grace
she releases my hand

*"Got your feet now, Poet?"* she asks

"Yes."

Before I can say thank you, she moves away from me
Back up the hillside to the camp
and the wounded

I recognize another figure standing further up the slope

Mercy raises her gloved hand to me
as she waits for Grace to catch up
I have a feeling those gloves were off a short while ago
and they have a great deal to do
with me standing on my feet
I look behind me
and find a peculiar sight there

Karma and Fate
Engaged in a heated discussion
I have no idea who is winning the argument
But Fate is NOT happy about something

And walking towards me
A vision in white

Pantheon

Hope

She approaches and
she pulls the golden laurel wreath
from her hair

As she reaches me
She raises it to her lips
and places a tender kiss upon it
before placing it in my hands

She reaches out her hand
to touch my cheek
She needn't say a word
her eyes tell me everything

As she walks past
I look down at the wreath in my hands
I am victorious

Eric Syrdal

# BACK TO THE BEGINNING: PART THE SECOND

Grace
Reminds me, that my legs are strong
She teaches me to stand when gravity and the weight of the world
would conspire to crush me.


Karma
Reminds me, though I may not withstand every attack
The actions I do in her name resonate through time
And will always return to defend me


Fate
Reminds me, when the wounds are deep and much blood is lost
I should remember that it is not my destiny to fail
Wounds heal but scars will always remain


Mercy
Reminds me, that I must keep striving to reach her
She only ever  touches me briefly and though it has the power
to calm the raging fire in my blood, she knows
I will need to live on to fight another day


Courage
Reminds me, that when I am afraid, she will always take my hand
and stand with me on the battle line. We may fall or we may be
victorious
Either way she will always restore my strength and my belief in
myself


Through the actions of all these Goddesses in my life
I am led to one more
I am led to you…


You are a fortress wrapped in warm skin, breathing life into my heart

# Pantheon

You remind me that misfortune and failure have no power over me
save what I give them
You stop the raging tempest of panic when I think about what
tomorrow might have in store for me
You are the promise on a dark night that I will see the sun again

You are Hope

# THE DRAGON
# AND
# THE DAMSEL

Eric Syrdal

# THE DRAGON AND THE DAMSEL
## I. Sonata

She has seen evidence
of the beast
everywhere around her
Through the streets
of the city
it leaves its evidence
on the grey landscape

Scorch marks on the concrete
broken scales on the playgrounds
teeth shattered and discarded
in the gutter
shades of green and brown
but often clear like ice

She hears its wings
scraping on the sides
of their tenement
at night
While everyone but she
is sleeping

She's heard its low growl
The heavy air of its presence
in the hallway
right outside her door

Pure of heart…

Her blood formed a natural
resistance to the beast

Pantheon

When the pressure of
the outside world bowed in
on her
The air would thicken enough
that she could hear its voice
speaking to her in rich whispers

But her life was solid and
secure behind the ramparts
she had spent the dearest
years of her existence building

And so…
she would go…
from gatehouse to field
from field to gatehouse
day in
day out
collecting her wages
from the lord of the land
Paying her tithe
to king and country

Feeding mouths which cannot feed themselves
saving the scraps for herself
Dining alone in the kitchen
When the rest of the world is in repose
fat and groggy on a full belly
Retiring herself to a lump-filled mattress
only when the hearts and breaths
of those around her
beat the slow rhythm of slumber

It is then,
In this time where dreams hang

Eric Syrdal

just out of reach

That the dragon speaks

A thin crack
no bigger than a length of
brown hair
from her head
will let it filter in

The voice…
like salted butter
on warm bread
aged and beautiful
like a rich wine
from ancient Greece
What harm could be done?

let it inside
let it crawl around the floor
under the kitchen table
around the chair
sleep on the window sill

It steals a small, reptilian kiss
from her lips
like a playful suitor…

Watching TV at 3am
Away from home and the hearts that need her
In the moments between heartbeats
When the world takes its accusing eyes off of her

A flicker of a forked tongue
and
a trickle of fire
down the throat

Serpentuously sliding itself
around her heart

purring there
until morning

Leaving no trace

Gentlemanly stealing away
before dawn
taking with it, the guest key
sweetly provided
and leaving in its place
a lovely note of:

"fond wishes and thank you for a lovely evening"

Flowery signature
punctuated with a long stem rose

And so it comes to pass
that the dragon and the damsel
purchase a delicate peace
and defer payment to a
nondescript weekday of the far future

Eric Syrdal

## THE DRAGON AND THE DAMSEL
## II. Largo

Brown eyes flutter open
The alarm clock
screeches
7:30 a.m.

Time to get moving
She hoists
herself up on an elbow
Shuffle of bed sheets
draws one leg up
reaching down to
massage the aching muscle
in her calf
She can feel
the empty space behind her
His side of the bed
It's been empty since 6
He left without kissing
her forehead
again
When he used to do
that
it always woke her up
for a brief moment
She has only been awakened
by the alarm
every day for weeks
She reaches over and slaps
at the off button…
Her eyes focus on
her right arm

Pantheon

Her full sleeve of tattoos

Asian feelings with modern styles
Koi in shades of reds and oranges
Dragon scales in shades of blues and greens
Peacock feathers and roses
Clouds and waves
Her mother always hated them
said it made her look like
a man; some kind of punk
He,
ever lifting her spirits
said that she was the
sexiest "man" he had ever seen

He used to hold her hand and look
at them for hours
always noticing more and more details
with each examination of them

Like visiting a priceless work
of art in a museum
She crosses the cold floor
in the bathroom…

The mirror
silent arbitrator of life's decisions
sentinel of self-doubt
a reflecting pool of unseen horrors
our accusatory doppelganger

Her image grins back at her
maniacal stare
brown eyes
haunting, vacant

but absolutely seething
with contempt
for them
for her
for life
dark bruises of weariness
beneath them
actual bruises
on her left cheek
When she fell
in the living room
getting up from the couch
chasing after him

After the argument
Her savage heart had raged
with scorching conviction
against his attempts to remove
the comforts she had found
that so easily allowed her to
shift the weight of the world
more evenly across her shoulders

She is always there
This woman in the mirror
She always has that same look in her eyes
that says,
Run
get away
be free of it…
You do not belong here
Go
You're killing us

Pantheon

As she moves down the hallway
she passes her cello
sitting neatly in its alcove
within the small apartment
from the day she moved in
it always claimed that spot

She plays
But not like she used to
Now when her fingers draw
the bow across the strings
the music she hears is only an
echo of what it used to be
She can only recall a few
of her favorite pieces
The largo from Dvorak's
New World Symphony
No.9
Almost unable to control
the welling of tears in her eyes
when she plays that one
such a gentle and soft melody
it echoes in her heart
or it used to

The last time she played it
was a few days ago

She had closed her eyes
and in her mind
She saw a woman
strong and powerful
in golden armor
Hair, black as midnight
Eyes, bluer than the deepest oceans

And for a while
she held the vision of this woman
in her mind
and she felt strength in her heart

Like she could be whole again
Like she could be free
Like she didn't need the dragon
It doesn't like that…
It shook the thought from her head

The music wavered and fell flat
The bow stopped
She put down her instrument
and forgot about the woman she saw
The dragon takes all but the most precious
of memories as its prize
Soon the memories of her music will
be no exception

Entering the kitchen
it was waiting for her

the beast
as it slumbers on the counter
its tail flowing across the floor
around the table and chairs
flicking playfully at her feet

The light outside
golden and bright
as the sun
climbed its ladder
to step over the horizon

Pantheon

She has brought with her
a dream
that she saved from last night

She found that lately
it required an offering
something precious and warm
from the dark of her mind
something of her older days

She places it on the counter
and so receives her reward
of dragon fire
to warm her heart and tired bones
on a crisp winter morning

Eric Syrdal

## THE DRAGON AND THE DAMSEL
## III. Intermezzo

Ear buds blaring

She hates the elevator
So many floors
to pass on the way down
So little room

In here

for them
for her

By the time she
reaches the street level
her nerves are spent
indents of her fingernails
in her palm

Doors open
She stands her ground
until all of them
have exited
including the guy
that was watching her
out of the corner of his eye

Every time they stopped
at another floor
to take on more souls
into her already capsizing
life boat
She retreated a little further
and a little further
back into the corner
Her winter coat
the only buffer between her
panic and the grimy walls

Pantheon

Earbuds in
take out the phone

Pull up the playlist
select another track
finger-slide

Max volume
Drown
It
Out
Step out of the front door

Icy wind hits like a sledgehammer
to the gut
The sun is blazing
but the wind
it cuts right through

The dragon fire
around her heart
gutters
Goes cold
Lies dormant and retreats from the sun
It always leaves when she needs
it the most

She could never
get used to the New York winter

It just seemed
to bury her
no matter how much snow
fell

The definition of insanity
Doing the same thing over and over
exactly the same way
and expecting different results

Like trying to learn that same piece of music she'd been struggling
with.
The one that tangled her fingers each and every time
Wanting to throw her bow across the room

Like trying to get pregnant
each time waiting for the test results
each time being crushed under that same rock

Like leaving a crowded elevator
To walk down a freezing city street
To go into an equally crowded coffee shop
…and it was packed today.

She waits
shifting her weight
Left foot
Right foot
10 ahead
5 ahead
her turn

Tables are mostly full
She pays her tithe and has her café mocha in hand

The tables are really full.
Maybe just go back to the apartment?

Head for the exit
Corner of her eye
Man folds his paper
Screeches his chair back on the tiles
Crumples his napkin and wipes away
donut crumbs from the table top

Small cocktail table
Two chairs
Now empty

She waits patiently

Pantheon

He starts off
makes eye contact
smiles, excuse me

She nods, smiles back
slides onto the seat
Cup in hand
Phone in the other…
Shop noise
the roar and squeal of the steamer
over conversation

Thumb-slide, open music app
Select: Playlist
Select: Escape Velocity
Select: Adagio for Strings
index finger, side button
"Warning: listening to music at high vol-"
Yeah…fuck off.
Max level

Now leaving Earth

Low, almost a whisper
The conversation is receding

She is the deepest part of the ocean

The notes start in the dark depths
Barely visible by the filtered sunlight
Bioluminescent flickers
Tiny electric fireflies
drifting ever upward

Power beyond any arcane explanation
They vibrate and hum with the strings
Gently floating up
Higher and higher

Until darkness gives way to twilight
Growing slowly brighter
The light of creation fusing with the music

Intensifying, broadening
Holding out its glowing arms to the
ever approaching surface

The bright topaz and shimmering greens
The warmth of our guardian star
Building stronger

Swelling chords of emotions
She feels the tight pinch at the back
of her throat
She has become the music
She is floating upward through
this warm, protective sea of emotions

Her heart is beating and she can feel it
Feel it above, above all else
This time, when she's with her music

At this one moment
The entire universe is reaching out to her
Consolation offered in the form
of audiocasted mercy

She turns her face upward
to meet the approaching sun
To break free of the surface as it looms
ever closer
To fill her lungs with oxygen
and new life

She doesn't feel the coffee cup
resting in her hand
Or the chair beneath her
Or her feet on the ground

She does feel the tear
escape the corner of her eye
eyes that are
closed tight and shutting out

the city
the people
the pain

It trickles to the edge of her jaw and hangs there
…with the last sustained notes

Then as someone bumps into the table
and sloshes hot coffee over the rim of
her cup and onto her hands

She is thrown back down
from heaven
into hell…

And like Lucifer

She screams in horror,
All the way down

A fiery comet of smoke and pinions
plunging back to the ocean's surface
to shatter her spirit there

Imprisoned by gravity
once more

Eric Syrdal

## THE DRAGON AND THE DAMSEL
## IV. Rondo

That feeling
when you can almost
reach out and touch
peace

That feeling doesn't
come to her often
Especially in these
last few months
The chord of her earbuds
had snagged on the
uppermost button of her coat

When she jerked her body
in startled reaction
as the hot coffee
touched the skin of her hand

The bulwarks in her ears popped out
and the outside world was waiting
Suddenly she was severed
from the music
From her only real form of escape
She was human again
and with her humanity comes
pain
and shame
and fear
and regret

The person who had caused
this train wreck
was still standing over her, hovering

Looking straight ahead
while dabbing at her hand
with a napkin,
she could see
the torso of a woman
Baggy jeans
the cuffs on the legs
were slightly scuffed
from being too long
and dragging the ground

A brown leather belt
through the loops
drawn tight against
her wide hips
and above that
some kind of sports jersey
peeked out from a
jacket of a golden material
that was slightly reflective
when turned just at the right angle
to the light

The woman was saying something

It sounded like an apology
repeated over and over
She was using a mundane
word

"Sorry"

How can such a ridiculously
simple word be used to
apologize for sentencing
someone back into this prison?

She had no concept of what she'd done

But it was hearing her name that
finally made her turn
her head up to look at the face of the
architect of this disaster
She was drawn to her eyes
immediately
They were deepest blue she had ever seen

They spoke of immense
understanding and kindness
and a fathomless strength
Her ebony hair
was pulled back in a ponytail
which gave her a youthful
appearance
Though the expression
on her face

one of concern and attention

seemed to convey a maturity
the likes of which her clothes and hairdo
could not exhibit

*"Angel? Are you ok?"*

Who was she? Did she meet her before and not remember?
Impossible
Her memory would certainly remember someone like this.
Firmly grounded back on earth now

She answered, "Yes. I'm fine. You just startled me. I'm ok."

The woman pulled out the chair
on the other side of the table
and sat down
pulling extra napkins
from her jacket pocket and holding them out

*"I'm so sorry. I guess I wasn't looking where I was going. Are you
hurt?"*

She took the napkins with a polite smile
not a friendly, so happy to see you, smile
it was a, thanks for worrying about me but I'm ok, smile
Shaking her head she sopped up the spilled coffee from the table top,
"No, I'm fine."

Her turn for a question, "Do I know you?"

The woman gave a smile now
and it was a genuine, happy to see you, smile
*"Yes, though we haven't spoken in a long time."*

Something was not adding up
the curiosity was wearing off
and she was starting to get that
nauseous feeling in her
stomach again

It had been with her since last weekend
almost every day

Sliding back her chair
leaving her coffee cup in
its place
she stood up and moved
to the side of the table

The woman watched her
but otherwise said nothing
Feeling the need to apologize
she opened her mouth
but quickly clamped it shut again
as a small hurricane swirled
in her stomach
The prospect of puking her guts up
in this small coffee shop
made her cheeks flush with embarrassment
turning
she headed for the door
Within arm's reach
of the threshold
the pressure of
holding back her
queasiness made her
head swim

She felt like the coffee shop
was spinning
like she was losing her balance
Then she was falling backward
Her arms shot out to the sides
to try and steady her

not working
gravity winning
going down

The last thing she remembers
is someone catching her from behind
in a very strong embrace

The radiator by the window
in the kitchen
makes a loud pinging noise
when it first comes on
It's a distinctive noise
she is used to hearing
when she's alone in the apartment
in the early mornings

As her eyes slowly open
she begins to realize
that is exactly where she is
She's sitting in the armchair next to the couch
in the living room

Her coat is on the hanger, next to the door
Her boots are sitting on the floor underneath
and she can see the glimmer of water
droplets on them from
the residual snow
She's been back for a little while
because the air
in the room doesn't have
that smell of "outside" it normally
does when she first gets back

Eric Syrdal

Looking at the couch next to her
also reveals

She's not alone
The woman from the coffee shop
sits, reclining back
arms folded over her chest
Only something is very different about her
She is wearing armor.

Suddenly it makes sense

She understands the familiarity
of the woman's face
She is the warrior
she's been seeing when
she plays her music

The woman with the deep
blue eyes, standing strong and firm
The woman whose image
seems to give her a strength
that denies her need for dragon fire
Someone from somewhere
who brings her
Courage

She licks the dryness from her lips and asks, "Who are you?"
A laugh
It hardly seems the time to laugh
but nonetheless she does
The woman sits up straight
armor plates sliding and clinking,

*"That, Angel, is a tricky question. The easiest answer…and the quickest to get us where we need to go today is; I am a part of you."*

Angel raises a hand to her forehead. The room isn't spinning any more but there is a dull ache there.
Kind of like a hangover, "Part of me?"

*"Yep. I've got so many names. I can tell you all of them but, I'll cut right to the chase with the one I am most fond of:  **Courage**."*

"Courage?"

*"Yes. You and I don't speak very often. But lately I've felt like you've been trying to. Something inside of you has been calling out to me. At a specific time when your soul is not so attached to this world. A time when you feel like you are free of everything here that hurts you."*

"When I play."

*"When you play.  When your cello is in your hands and you aren't here on this rotting dust ball.  You aren't on earth. You are somewhere else. That is when I'm able to hear you. And you've been pleading for me to come. So now I'm here."*

Courage stands and moves closer to the arm chair.
Angel's eyes are closed
her hand rests against her temple
gently rubbing at the pain there

To anyone else,
she's just a very tired woman
sitting in a chair after an exhausting experience

But what Courage can see, makes her blue eyes shimmer with an intense flame

and produces a white-hot tear
that drips down her cheek

Coiled around the chair
across Angel's chest
Her arms at the wrists
Her legs at the ankles
Slithering and grotesque
around her shoulders and her neck…
scales
talons
frilled and fin-like
dripping with disdain
Contempt
Pain
Misery
And with a gaping maw
filled with needle sharp teeth
beneath a muzzle with smoldering
nostrils of acrid smoke

…eyes flicking with balefire
growling and hissing
angry and spiteful…
The dragon makes its presence known

With a voice that breaks as it begins, Courage speaks, "*In all our years of togetherness. In all the times as a little girl, your heart called me to your side to chase away the imaginary monsters under your bed. I never thought I would come to find you so grown up and in such a desperate need to make an alliance with a real monster. My sweet Angel. What have you done?*"

"What have I done?" she answers, "What I've needed to do to
survive. It makes me stronger.  It helps me live with myself. When no
one else will. It keeps my heart warm when I feel like it will freeze."

Courage kneels next to her chair and takes her hand
It's cold

And as she reaches for Angel's fingers, the coils of the dragon
retreat from her touch
It gives a soft growl
like a cat
that's being tormented and wants
to be left alone
She squeezes Angel's hand
in her grip, another tear dripping from her cheek,

*"Angel. You don't need this creature to help you. You're stronger
than this. WE are stronger than this."*

Angel shakes her head slowly
The dragon slides its coils
tighter around her chest
causing her to gasp a little

It bares its fangs at the woman
in the golden armor
A warning:
**THIS IS MINE**

Courage wipes another tear
from her eyes
She leans her head down
to touch her forehead
against the back of Angel's hand

The dragon recoils further
releasing some of its grip
in an effort to move as far from
the warrioress as possible
without letting go of its prey


*"Angel, I want to remind you of someone we both know. A young girl,
who grew up in a very hard place. Her life was never easy..."*

Angel nods slightly and speaks, "...but she was determined to become
a musician."
Courage continues, *"...and she did...and went as far and as high as
she could go inside of that small town where she grew up."*

Angel smiles, "That little town orchestra...playing concerts on
Christmas and the 4th of July..."

Courage looks up, tears falling harder and faster...
The dragon,
very angry now,
loosens another coil from Angel's ankle and arm
It slips partially back across the floor
Still within striking distance
growling and hissing louder
It tries to stare down Courage,
the balefire in its eyes flaring brighter

She wipes another tear with her free hand, *"...but always dreaming.
She always kept her dreams close to her heart. One day, she would
get the opportunity of a lifetime..."*

Angel nods, "...an invitation to try out for the New York
Philharmonic..."

Courage continues, "...*So she packs up her things. Says goodbye to her family and heads east....*"

"She's afraid..."

"*...But she's strong...and she makes that long trip across the country all by herself...*"
Angel's eyes finally focus on Courage's eyes, "...and she made it...she got here and she auditioned and she made it... she's finally part of her dream. It's real and she can feel it. Touch it..."
The dragon releases its hold completely and retreats to the back of the room.
scales standing up on end around its haunches

It roars and it hisses
It even sprays out a few gouts of flame to singe the floor nearby

Courage smiles, "*...and she is stronger than that thing.*" she jerks her head in the direction of the beast

Suddenly, Angel's eyes lose focus
Her head looks down into her lap
and she shakes it slowly from side to side

"The woman you describe is gone. She hasn't been here for a long, long, time."

Emboldened by this response
the dragon takes a step forward

If it is possible for a beast to smile
it would be smiling

It begins to make its way back over to the chair
To the figure sitting in it
with hunched shoulders
with the fire that was there only moments ago
slowly dying in her heart

She's calling for the dragon fire to warm her
and it's going to answer

Courage is on her feet
still holding Angel's hand

She hauls her up out of the chair
The movement startles her out of her stupor
The dragon, retreats back a step again
unsure of where this is going…
Courage puts her arm around
Angel's waist
positions her alongside of her
to offer as much support as she can
She speaks into her ear
softly but firmly

*"I have something to show you, come on"*

Together they head to the bathroom.

Angel has spent agonizing minutes
each day
looking into that mirror
and now she was being confronted
with it again

*"Look."* Courage said

and gestured towards the glass

But when Angel did
It was different…

Instead of seeing the reflection
of her own bathroom
it was the reflection of someone else's bathroom
Who?
She wasn't certain
But she would find out soon enough
as a young man came into the room
on the other side
turned on the light and made his way
over to the mirror.

He leaned on the sink
his sink
on the other side
He was young
probably late 20's
pale skin
but dark brown hair
and eyes
The skin around them was
red and puffy
He'd been crying recently
only moments ago
Now he seemed to be looking
at his reflection
She'd seen that look a thousand times
in the reflection of her own face
doubt
fear

pity
anger
and most of all
hate

His eyes flicked back and forth
a few times
as if he was focusing on each of
his own eyes in turn
left, right
right, left
Searching for an answer
that wasn't there

Angel knew it wasn't there
she'd looked for it every day too
"Who is he?"
she said, as the young man dropped his face down to
look at the sink
showing the two women the top of his head
and shoulders that were collapsing under whatever
unseen weight he was carrying..

*"His name is Alexander."* Courage finally answered *"He's 28 years old and he's in medical school. He's just finished a long day of lectures and he's back at the small apartment where he lives off campus."*

"Why is he so sad?" asked Angel…reaching out a hand to touch the glass of the mirror

*"Because he has no reason to be happy, Angel. None at all. The universe has turned its back on him."*

"What happened?"

*"He lost his father 3 years ago to cancer. A subject he studies a lot about. He's planning on becoming an oncologist. He's got a few years left. He's far away from his home and family so he wasn't able to be there the day his father passed. Things were beginning to look up for him in this last year until a few weeks ago, when he lost his fiancée in a car accident.*
*He was studying very late and she wanted to go to a concert. He told her he was too tired. They had an argument. She decided to go with some of her girlfriends. One of them was drunk and decided to drive home.....The accident was terrible and killed all of them. He blames himself.*
*As you can imagine, he hasn't been able to concentrate on his work...which means his grades are failing...he will more than likely need to drop out of school next semester.*
*As far as he is concerned...his life is over. "*

"But it's not. Right?"  Angel looks over her shoulder where Courage is standing just inside the doorway
Courage shrugs. Armored plates scraping with the movement.
*"I don't think so..."*

Angel's attention is drawn back to the young man by some movement of his image. He reaches forward and opens the medicine cabinet taking a small brown bottle and emptying a bright red pill into his palm. He fills a cup with some water and takes the pill, quickly swallowing it down.
"What's that?"

*"His dragon."* Replies Courage. *"He's been able to hold on this long because of it. A prescription he was able to get from a friend, who has a friend, who has a friend. . ."*

Angel nods, "Is it an addiction?"

*"Not completely yet, no. It's just started to get its coils around him. But he'll break free because of you."*

Angel backs away from the mirror with a confused look on her face, "Because of me?"

*"Yes,"* Courage answers, *"and when he does, through his work, he will be responsible for one of the greatest breakthroughs in human history."*

"My God! You mean? He cures cancer?"

Courage chuckles, *"No. But his research leads to a development by a team of scientists who create a drug that does."*

A long moment passes as Angel tries to process this information. When she finally speaks her voice has a stronger quality, "What do I have to do with this?"

*"Everything."* Replies Courage as she steps over to her, *"A few moments from now he will decide to call his mother. Just to talk. A last plea for help. And he'll find it. When she tells him a story about a woman she knew who was at the end of hope and reached deep inside herself and found a strength she never knew she had. How she found out that day that she never needed the dragon to begin with. That all she ever needed was deep inside her own heart just waiting to be uncovered."*

Several more moments pass as Angel continues to process what she is being told.
Courage stands in front of her, very close.

"Courage, are you telling me? Is this? Is this my son?"

A chuckle, *"No, Angel he's not your son."*

"Then…who-?"

Courage reaches out her hand and gently nestles it against Angel's
abdomen just below her belly button.
*"Hers"*

Angel's hand moves over to cover Courage's

"You mean? I'm?"

Courage smiles a broad smile that covers her entire face. *"Yes. About
6 weeks. With a little baby girl that will one day have a son who she
will name Alexander. Who will one day call her on a desperate night
so she can tell him a story.  A story about her mother. A story about
you, here and now…in this moment."*

A fierce roar
louder than a building coming down
echoes from the living room
It shakes the walls
and the mirror

Courage continues to smile as she hears the noise.
*"OOhhhhhhh….somebody doesn't like that very much."*

Angel, still a little in shock, nods her head and looks to the doorway

There is a light in her eyes now
but it doesn't come from dragon fire
It's the light of herself
She clenches her jaw and nods a few times
as if affirming a question
she has been asking herself
for a long time

Courage nods and draws her sword, *"Fate  is going to be furious with me…but you know what? I think it was worth it."*

She holds the sword out
Handle first
for Angel to take it
Which she does
Feeling the weight of
the weapon in her hands
Her hands
in control of her own fate
for once
She'll live or die by her own choice
Not the whim of some foul creature

A creature that feeds off her need to be
successful
important
useful

Another sound
from the living room…

This time it's not a roar
No
It is a sorrowful
pitiful howl
of an animal that is realizing
it's just been cornered
and the odds of escaping
with its life
are not good…

"Never heard that before," says Angel, as she takes her first steps towards the door sword in hand.

Courage smiles, *"All this time you've heard what it sounds like when it's in control. When it's on top. Now…for the first time, dear Angel, you will know what it sounds like when it is afraid. And it is. It's afraid of you."*

And together
they step through
the doorway to engage
in a battle,
the outcome of which,
is not only a victory for one woman's soul
but for the soul of mankind.

# AMOR VINCIT OMNIA

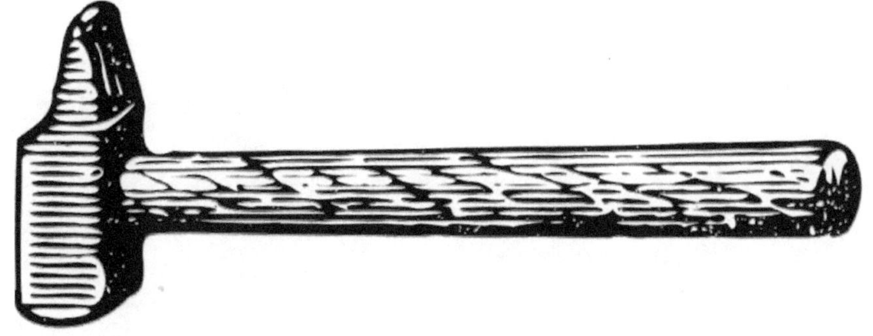

# AMOR VINCIT OMNIA

## I.

Amor Vincit Omnia
Love Conquers All
Is that phrase true?
I can attest that it
is very true in most cases…
That with the presence of love
Life finds it very hard indeed to allow sadness and misery to prevail

But what about Fate?
Do you believe in her?
Do you believe that she is ruled by such an edict?
Would you believe
that there was a time
when she was?

We all know her
Indeed, perhaps she is the very reason that you are here
for me to tell this tale

Maybe, alone in her forge,
she decided
amid red-hot irons and flying sparks
that you were to be here
to understand this story
about her

Maybe you had no choice
but to be here
as I
have no choice
but to tell this story to

anyone and everyone who
may listen…

To help you to comprehend
To understand
that while she may seem cruel
and unfeeling to you
It was not always thus….
To begin…
It is important that you understand

The Queen of Hearts
is a sister to
Courage, Karma, Mercy, Grace, Hope and yes, even Fate

She moves them each in kind…
The Queen
is love
and as such holds dominion over
them all…

Love begets Courage
Love directs Karma
Love inspires Mercy
Love speaks of Grace
Love is the basis for Hope
But what of Fate?

Powerful arms,
molded by sweat and toil
tanned skin
by the heat of the forge
and the strike of the hammer

Hair, entangled in the golden sun
Eyes, greener than the elysian fields
But her heart?
The biggest of all hearts
A heart big enough to encompass
all of mankind
to love each and every face she sees
each and every soul that she shapes
and to shed tears for each and every name
that appears in The Great Book

Each name that she reads
once on the day of our birth
and a second time
when the curtain closes
on the final performance
of our role
in this never-ending saga

There was a time
when love ruled Fate
When Fate cared…
When she was the first one
to begin our standing ovation
and the last to leave the theatre
in tears…

This is the story of that time…
…and how it all changed

The story
of how the immortal architect
of our future
read a name

that appeared in The Great Book
for the first time
The name of a mortal man
And by seeing his entire existence
laid out before her eyes
allowed herself to feel
allowed herself to fall…
to fall, in love
to make that same harrowing
plummet we take so much for granted
as it quickens the pulse of our mortal hearts

But you and I
stumble blindly into love
know nothing of the future
of the ones we choose to give our hearts to

We live each day
as though it was a new page
in a book yet to be read
sometimes, yet to be written

We are not goddesses…
Most of all, we are not Fate
Would you do it?

Would you allow yourself to fall
in love
with someone whose future
you know
with someone whose entire life
is laid out before your preternatural eyes
day by day

You can see
all their triumphs
all their successes
all their weak moments
all their failures
all the days of their lives
and how they will die

Would you accept those visions
and allow
all things to happen as written?
Or do you pick up the pen
and edit the story?
Do you
break the rules?

## AMOR VINCIT OMNIA
## II.

The palace is not just a structure…
Some say it is
a living, breathing, thing…

It is said
if you lay your ear
against the flagstones
you can hear the sound
of a heartbeat

Of course it's fitting
that the Queen resides here
under its sweeping arches
glorious ramparts
glittering stones
blood red and golden banners
waving in the midday sun

Fate entered the throne room
through its heavy oaken door
Beams of sunlight cast down
through stained glass windows
making gorgeous patterns
upon the crimson carpet
that dominated the center
of the circular room
6 Thrones carved of pale wood
sat

3 to each side
of a massive seventh
centered and

slightly raised on a dais
to be about a foot taller than the others

Near
those seats of power
stood a grouping
of their owners
An assembly of
the Queen's court
Fate's sisters

They flocked to her
immediately as she entered…
a flurry of colored fabrics
a kaleidoscope of skin tones
a symphony of vocal arpeggios
rising and falling
with excitement and pleasant greetings
at their sister's arrival

Fate
constructed a smile
fashioned a pleasant tone
in her voice
and with her hammer hanging
from her right hand at her thigh
exchanged one-armed warm hugs
and gentle kisses of affection
with her siblings

But she understood
that to be in this room
was to be at the service of the Queen
and they had business
to discuss

and
no sooner
had the thought left her mind
then the doors at the far end
of the throne room opened
and with all the regal splendor
accompanying her title
the Queen entered

Powerful and tall
her presence poured
into the room

Upon her arrival
at the palace
most of her armor
had been removed
replaced with long
and lavish layers of gowns
all in various shades of red
from scarlet to crimson
from apple to rose

A golden tiara
on her head
stretched out long
tendrils of stylized sun rays
reaching from a central medallion
in the shape of a heart
it wove its way
between the deep
orange-red waves of her hair

Under the inferno of her mane
her freckled face

radiated her beauty like
a torch throwing its light
upon the surface of water

Her ice blue eyes
fixed upon the assembly
before the thrones
and there was a loud "shoosh"
of movement
as her six sisters
genuflected in unison

A miniature tempest
of attendants and servants
flooded in behind her
two moved quickly to the central throne
depositing banners
into stands upon the floor to either side
One, a battle standard
depicts
the armored form
of the Queen
standing upon a winged
creature personifying
sorrow

Its wings tattered and broken
it claws at the ground beneath it
trying desperately to escape her
she carries a sword
poised to strike at the creature's neck
and deliver a death-blow

The other,
which frequently flies

from the highest tower
of the castle
is a single red heart
on a pure white field
it is the personal seal
of the Queen herself

The other attendants
take positions around the room
standing at attention
When she speaks
her voice is not a light feather
floating to the floor from heaven
Neither is it a deep rolling thunder
It is calm
and even
and strong
and potent with a matter-of-factness
that makes it almost
impossible to
contradict her

"Sisters, please, arise and be welcome within the walls of this place."

There was another soft shooshing as the court rose to their feet

Instantly, Mercy crossed the floor to stand before her. "My Lady?
What of our Poet?"

The Queen smiled
as she removed
her riding gloves
and held them out to the side.
An attendant moved quickly
to retrieve them

"He is well and will return to us in due time." She smiled

A collective sigh
of relief was breathed
by the assembled court
Mercy clasped her
gloved hands together
and nodded a silent "thank you"

The Queen continued. "He had traveled quite far and, as is his way,
he requires some time to journey back to the palace. But you should
all feel confident that he will reunite with us on the battlefield very
soon."

"I told you, he would" spoke a voice from the group.

Grace
swarthy skinned
and with a beauty that underscores
her name
stepped forward into the Queen's presence
her dark eyes
combined with her
genuine smile
produced a smile of
like kind
from the Queen

"Indeed you did, Gentle Grace" said the Queen, "My dispatch to
retrieve him was only in the interest of time."

Her pale eyes traveled
from Grace's smile
to where Fate stood
Head down...in contemplation

"Speaking of time," she continued, "Dear Fate, I am to understand
you requested an audience with me?"

Fate's shoulders
slumped down
as if a ton of bricks
had been hefted upon her

For such a powerful and striking
specimen of strength and form
her profile seemed small now
a tiny flicker
of the roaring flame
she was known to be

As if it were a funeral march
she began
making her way to
the Queen
her head did not look up
her eyes did not see anything but the floor
as she journeyed
in silence

As she came to rest in front of her, the Queen spoke, "Dearest Sister.
What is it that troubles you so? What would you ask of me? Speak…
and give me your eyes and your beautiful face to answer to."

Fate looked up
finally allowing the
green meadows of
her eyes to meet
the blue skies
of her sovereign sister's

Her powerful bicep
lifted her strong arm
with her skilled hand
encircled around
the haft
of her hammer
She held it out
before the Queen
as if a child
offering a wildflower
to their beloved mother
Her deep voice was barely a whisper, "My Lady. I must forswear my
hammer. I remit it to your custody…and ask that you release me from
your court."

The Queen
her mouth agape
and though of pale skin
looking paler still
almost could not form
the words to ask

"My sweet sister. Of course I refuse. What power has sent you thus to
me and draped such a dark shroud over your spirit? What turns your
emerald eyes to coal and has stolen the sunlight from your hair?"
And with a heavy sigh and a tear at the corner of the eye, Fate
responded
"Love"

## **AMOR VINCIT OMNIA**
## **III.**

There is a silence…

Not the ordinary quiet
moments
of the normal day
when rooms muffle noises
of the outside world
nothing is ever truly
quiet…
noise levels
may be reduced
in such a way
that you feel like
you can't hear anything
But there is always
something in the background…
The wind
The rumble of cars on a nearby highway
The low hum of an air conditioning system
The slow and steady thrumming of
your own heartbeat

Believe me when I tell you
there was no sound within that
room

or the next room…

or the outside world…

Fate and the Queen
spent

what felt like an eternity
standing before each other

The hammer
held out at arm's length
would have dropped
back to the side
of any mortal man I know
The weight of it
and the reason it was offered
would have dragged the
head back down
to point at the earth

Gravity…
would have mercifully ended
what can only be
described
as an excruciatingly uncomfortable
situation

But it was only the voice of the Queen
that allowed everyone
in that room to finally take another breath
"Everyone. Please allow Fate and I to talk alone." she said.
No one answered
At least not with their voices
there was a flurry of movement
a bow or a curtsy
and then the throne room
fell silent once more

The Queen
turned away from
Fate

and wandered over
to stand at the
foot of the main
throne
with her back to her sister
Her gowns
flowed along with her
like some
wispy sea creature
in multiple shades
of red
that drifts across the ocean floor

Fate
standing in a circle
of crystalline colors
from the stained glass
understanding that
her offering
was not to be accepted
let the hammer fall back
against her thigh
She took
a long, deep breath
and wiped a tear
away with the back of her
free hand

The Queen's voice filled the chamber again, "We spend time with
them, Fate."

Fate answered softly, "My Lady?"

"Mortals. We spend time with them don't we?" she sighed,

"Some of us more than others."

Fate nodded, "We do."

The Queen
turned to look at her sister again
This time though
her face had
a much different expression
one would almost call it pity, or better still,
remorse

"I'll admit" she offered, "That some of us aren't always needed. So
we only really spend time with them when we are necessary. We
offer them what we can… and then" she gestured around her, "we
return here. Until we are called on again."

She held out her hands to her sister as a gesture for her to approach.
"But you, Dear Fate. You are with them their entire lives. You know
them from start to finish. You know each one of their joys and pains
intimately. So your heart is the most vulnerable."

Fate moved across the floor to her sister. Her eyes scanned the
Queen's face for some understanding.
She hadn't explained herself
but she had a feeling
that her story needn't
be recited….

As if in answer to her silent question, the Queen explained. "I know
every heart that exists, Sister. Even yours. When I look there I can see
what it is that hurts you so."

"Forgive me, My Lady. I did not mean for this to happen."

The Queen smiled, "Of course not, dear. It was bound to happen sooner or later. Though we are not mortal, we still feel emotion. It is only natural that love be one of those emotions."

Fate nodded a few times

The Queen continued, "We are all capable of love, Sister. Were it not for love, would I so zealously chase down our wayward poet?" she laughed, "And I can tell you that Karma is quite fond of him too…as is Courage, for that matter."

She took Fate's hand in hers holding it palm up between them.  "Your hands are rough from the work you do, Fate. And it is so very important. But with these same rough hands you are capable of such sweet acts of selfless affection. We do not choose to love whom we do…But we must love according to our roles. And respect the boundaries within those roles"

The Queen looked deep into Fate's eyes, "Love is love, sister Fate. And we may choose freely of love so long as it does not break our role. Yours most sincerely of all."

Fate pulled back her hand
curling her fingers into a fist
and holding it
against her chest
Her emotions were
held at bay
for the longest time
as her sister spoke
of love being free
and a worthy treasure
for the taking
When the talk
moved back to

the importance of
her duty
her resolve shattered
into a million teardrops
of pain
Distraught
by Fate's recoiling
the Queen
pressed for an answer

"My Sister," she said, "What makes you pull away from my touch
so? Surely you know there is nothing you can do that would make me
renounce you so harshly as to want to be free of your touch?"

Fate answered, with a quiver in her voice, "It isn't what I would
do…it is what I have done."

## **AMOR VINCIT OMNIA**
## **IV.**

It was that feeling…

Like when
lightning strikes
so close
that it lights
up the world around
you like a spotlight
And you know
it's coming…
You know
the thunder is
going to be so loud
so violent
that it is going
to shake you to
your very core
it's going to
hurt your ears
and stop your heart
you want to
fall on the ground
and curl up into a ball
slam your palms against
your ears and squeeze
your eyes shut
so hard
that you can feel the skin
on your cheeks stretching…

You're panicking
Your mind is racing

You're thinking of all
the things that might happen
Is it going to hurt?
Will my family know what
happened to me?
Am I going to die?
But
what your primitive
instincts are drowning out…
what your flight or fight response
has temporarily erased…
is that you've seen the lightning
So when the thunder comes
It can't possibly mean
all the bad things
you are conjuring in your head

In these milliseconds
when your heart is racing
you've forgotten
one very important thing
If you hear the thunder…
Everything is ok…
Because you are still alive…
Fate saw
the lightning
of what she had done…
Now
all she needed to do
was tell the story
and wait for her sister's thunder…
A moment
to collect her thoughts
and then she opened
the gates to her

heart and let it spill
onto the floor…

"He was an engineer onboard a starship. Doing his job, in a war, that no one remembered the reasons behind. He was good at his job. His ship was ambushed by an enemy fleet. Despite his best efforts it sustained enough damage to cripple it. They were boarded and everyone left alive was taken prisoner.

He, along with 200 other prisoners, was being transferred to a prison camp in enemy controlled space. There was an accident, in the drive section, of the transport ship. Poison gas and radiation were flooding the lower decks including the brig where the prisoners were being held.

A riot ensued, and several prisoners were able to take down the enemy guards in the panic-stricken chaos. They broke free of their cells and made their way to the upper decks of the ship except for him. He headed into the drive section to shut down the containment leak. Amid the radiation and poisonous fumes, he shut down the reactor and sealed off the decks that were contaminated. Two thirds of the crew, including some of his fellow prisoners, survived because his last moments of life were a series of selfless acts.

Of course, I knew the outcome. I'd seen it long before he was able to walk or talk. I watched and waited. I listened to him calling for Mercy…in his mind. His lungs were shredded. He had radiation burns over most of his body.  He was blind and couldn't speak. He was in agony but his spirit was strong. His body kept fighting to stay alive. No one could sustain that much damage and survive. It would be over soon. Or so I thought. But he kept holding on. He kept willing his heart to beat even though he couldn't breathe. He was alone… helpless… afraid… and dying an agonizing death but his soul was shining like an inferno against the nothingness between the stars.  I

could feel the hundreds of other souls on the decks above him calm
and relieved.
He had done that.
He had put their minds at ease.
He had saved them."

Fate looked at her sister and almost smiled. "My Lady, I was moved
by his sacrifice. He was a hero…and so few of them ever are. I tried
to leave. Believe me when I say, I tried to leave him there…in pain
and misery… until his body finally gave out. And I knew that it
would. Unless…"

The Queen shook her head
it was her turn to look down
at the floor

She spoke quietly, "Sister please no… you didn't…"

Fate continued, "Unless I stopped it. Unless I used this…" she laid
her hand on the head of her hammer, "to build him a different
ending."

The Queen looked up
and met Fate's emerald gaze again.
A brilliant light
had been lit there.

She wanted
to suddenly be deaf…
Wanted to not be able to hear
the words she knew were
coming…

"And I did."

Now
silence reigned again
Fate could feel the weight
of what she'd done
but it had been lifted from
her shoulders
for once
she could feel it sitting there
on the ground in front
of her

It was like sitting
in a boat
on the surface of the ocean
with something
like a leviathan
ancient and massive
sitting below the water
underneath you
and then
it burst through
the surface
in the form of
the Queen's voice

"Fate, my Precious Sister"

"I know"

"Fate, we can't…"

"I know"

"Can you see a future for him, now?" she turned her back to
Fate, walking away toward the center of the room again.

"No."
"Nothing since you saved his life?"

"No."

"What have you done?"

"It will be ok, won't it? I didn't leave anything behind. No evidence at all. It'll be a medical miracle…They'll say what they always do. It wasn't his time yet…"

"BUT IT WAS HIS TIME, FATE!" The Queen spun to face her sister again and her voice echoed in the throne room.

Fate stood still
Shoulders clenched tight
against the force of
her sister's words
When she answered
it was even-tempered
a genuine pleading tone…
"Forgive me, My Lady…I didn't mean t-"

"I know," The Queen nodded, "I know you didn't, Fate. It was foolish of me to believe that in all this time, you were immune to the things that move our hearts."

She walked forward until she was close enough to embrace her sister. Her arms looked delicate next to Fate's but they held just as much strength. They were sisters and would share this burden together…. But Fate…was still waiting for the thunder…

## **AMOR VINCIT OMNIA**
## **V.**

The thunder shook
the plexiglass window
echoing like a bass drum
inside the small
hab unit

She sat
facing the window
one leg curled up under her
the other bent at the knee
with her thigh resting
against her chest

Storms
everyday here
they were terra-forming
this world
the atmospheric processors
belched water vapor
into the sky
saturating it with moisture
when met with warmer
or cooler winds
all manner of storms
were created
Some
violent and destructive
Some
light and mundane
This one
had been much
more aggressive earlier
now
it had quieted
to a deep rumble of
thunder every now and again

and a steady
downpour of rain

She watched
the drops collect
on the window
watched them run down…
they each started as
individuals
taking a path of chaos
down the glass
Along the way
they would come close
to each other

Sometimes
they would join up
and become a bigger drop
like couples meeting

Sometimes
those bigger drops
meet up with others
like families

Sometimes
the drops separate again
and drift far away from each other
like tragedies

But they all ended
in one large puddle
at the bottom of
the window

They all combined
to form a single
rippling pool
made up of every drop

that had traveled
down the window so far

The experience
of each journey
in one large reservoir
of combined knowledge

Each journey had a story
Each drop could tell of
meetings
or being alone
or of imperfections
in the craftsmanship
of the length of glass
it traveled

Every story
had a beginning
a middle
and an end
With truth, lies, and details along the way

That's how their lives
were built…
Mortals
That's how their lives were constructed
Beginning
Middle
End
And the end is final
In her hands
the cup of coffee
sent slender
streams of steam into the air
in front of her
face

She hadn't
touched it in hours

the microscopic
filaments running
through the porcelain
kept it just as hot
as it had been when she
received it from the beverage console

Behind her
in the dark of the hab-room
she heard
his breathing change pace
he was waking up

Thunder rumbled again
A gentle reminder of why she was here
What she had to do

She waited until
she heard him moving around
before she set the cup
down on the table
next to her
and turned the chair to
face the bed
He was reclining on one elbow
rubbing away at his left eye
with the back of his hand
He wasn't an
unattractive man…
He also wouldn't fall
in the category of Adonis-like

But that's not how
she perceives mortals anyway

She does not see
cheeks with a few days of stubble
hair, scattered and pointing in every direction
chest lacking defined pectorals
morning breath

Pantheon

She sees
The first time he cut himself shaving
His worry that his hair is falling out too fast for his age
His embarrassment at his poorly defined muscles and his stomach
sticking out a little
His mind estimating whether he should leap out of bed to brush his
teeth before asking for a kiss…

She sees moments
of us…

All of them…
At our worst and at our best…
And at the center of all she sees of him
she sees that moment when she
saved him
10 years ago

When she made a choice
dictated by her heart
and according to her sister
a mistake of epic proportions
that had only one answer
for how it should be corrected….

She smiles to herself
as she catches
a glimpse of what
he is thinking

A flash of skin
words spoken in breathless whispers
snapshots of their love-making
just hours before

His voice
travels across the room
clearly…

"Why are you awake so early?"

She answers, *"Can't sleep."*

"Bad dream?"

She nods, *"Something like that."*

In the half-light of the room,
she sees him
slide from under the sheets
to sit at the foot of the bed
a few feet away from her…

"Want to talk about it?" He asks

She shakes her head no.

"Ok." He nods, "Well I had an amazing dream." He yawns and rests
his elbows on his knees.

Fate looks at him with a raised eyebrow, *"Oh yes?"*

"Yep. About that time you and I were hiking in the Blue Ridge
Mountains on Earth. When we got stuck in that thunderstorm near
that abandoned cabin." He gestures to the window, "Rain must have
reminded me."

Fate nods a few times and reaches a hand up to tuck a golden tuft of
hair behind her ear.

He continues, "We were soaked…took all our clothes off and built a
fire in the corner out of that old furniture. Remember?"

She nods.

"I remember each and every raindrop on your body that day and how
good it felt to hold you in my arms while I kissed each one of them
away from your shoulders, your back" he sighed, "And your breasts.
All the parts of that amazing body of yours"

She smiles.

He gives a long pause, "I still don't understand what you are doing with a guy like me. You could have any man you want" He looks down at the floor, then back at her, "I'm just so thankful we met. I mean there you were standing in that hospital room. I survived a horrible ordeal and there you were, like an angel. Just waiting to take me away with you. And we've been together ever since. Fate really must have known what she was doing when she brought us together."
A thunder-clap
louder than any other
so far
rattles the window again
echoing into the distance
but it keeps rolling
moving
reminding

She answers, "*No, Love. She didn't*"

Not an answer he was expecting
confused
he thinks maybe she is setting up a joke

"What are you talking about?" he laughs nervously, "Of cou-"

"*She didn't know what she was doing.*"

And now he's silent
A sharp pain starts
in the pit of his stomach
his palms begin to sweat

"Come on now. What are you saying?" he asks

"*She didn't know.*" says Fate as she unfolds herself from the chair. She moves around to stand in front of him. Looking down at his face and her eyes are more serious than he has ever seen them.

She continues, "*She saw you there. On the prison ship and she followed you. When you broke that guard's nose and took the key off his belt. When you threw it to the others and told them to free the rest.*

*When you moved down the hallway, klaxons blaring!! Warning lights flashing. Pointing the safe direction to go. And you went in the opposite direction to save them"*

He looks at her,
confused
She's mentioned a few things
he's never mentioned to her….
but he doesn't interrupt.

*"She saw how you were starting to panic and how your mind was begging for you to go back the other way. But you wanted to shut down the core. You wanted to seal off the decks. You knew there was no way you were going to get out of this but you wanted them to make it. She watched you punch button after button on the consoles. Following shut down procedures. She heard your mind screaming in agony as the poisonous gas was filling your lungs. How you thought it was strange that it kind of smelled just like those tropical flowers that used to grow in your mom's backyard"*

His eyes suddenly went wide
He opened his mouth
to say something
but found that he couldn't

Fate had closed her eyes now, as if reciting from memory, *"You used to hate those things. Fate was there with you after you shut everything down. When you were in so much pain and all you wanted was to live. She watched you fight to struggle through the pain. Trying to stay alive. And she had never seen something so beautiful in all her life. You call it willpower and it was amazing to see. Your entire body shining like a beacon against the universe. You were heroic. And so very few people actually are! You were genuine. You were you."*

Fate opened her eyes, *"I…had never seen anything like that before."*

In order for her
to be near him

it had been necessary for her
to suppress her spirit…
It was absolutely necessary….
Because…
when mortals are near it
they know.
They get a feeling that they
are near something;
powerful
older than ancient
Unnatural…

She removed
the invisible mask
she had been wearing
all this time
to spare his gentle soul…
And he knew…
Instantly and without any doubt
he knew….
And he can see her
Really see her
And he knows what she did for him….
And he knows who she is….
More importantly he knows why she is here…
And he's terrified…

He stands
and Fate reaches
out to cup his shoulders
in her strong hands

He looks to her
hand and then back to her face
His voice is trembling so badly, it would be barely coherent to anyone
but her.

She can hear him clearly, "…it was you?….You're the one who
saved me?"

She answers, "*Yes.*"

"And you're here with me now, because that was a mistake? And you have to correct that mistake?"

"*Yes.*"

"So you kept me alive, only to let me die now?"

Her expression shows how painful the answer is, "*It's my fault…all my fault…I never wanted this to end like this. I'm so sorry.*"

He is breaking
down into tears….
He would have collapsed a long time ago
if it were not for her holding him up….
She pulls him into an embrace and she can feel him shuddering like a
building in the throes of an earthquake…

She speaks softly into his ear, "*I never knew what love was until I met
you. I was selfish… and I changed your ending to suit my own
needs.  You know who I am. You know why I can't let this continue.
You know why I am not allowed to love.*"

His voice was fading…
His body was succumbing to her embrace…
But he managed to say one last thing
before air would no longer fill his lungs…
"Please don't do this, Fate… I love you."

And she answered as she slowly lowered his lifeless body back to the
bed,

"*I know, Love…and you are probably the last person…who ever
will.*"

## AMOR VINCIT OMNIA
## VI.

Tragic Hero:

Defined: A **tragic hero** is a person of noble birth with **heroic** or potentially **heroic** qualities. This person is fated by the Gods or by some supernatural force to doom and destruction or at least to great suffering. But the **hero** struggles mightily against this fate and this cosmic conflict wins our admiration.

This simple explanation
pulled from
a data stream…
Packets of information
flying at light speed
through wires
and circuits
in a machine language
that forms them
on a screen
or transfers them
to a page…
A *simple* explanation
constructed by *simple* life forms
in a complex universe…
A hero
struggling against fate
But what if that hero *is* Fate?
What if she's the one who's doomed?
What if she's the one we watch
with an aching heart
trying valiantly
but foolishly

to circumvent
the inevitable…

Do we see her
as a hero?
Do we see her
as a villain?

Or will you see her as I tell you about her now?

She entered the throne room
to no grand fanfare
No trumpets
heralded her return to the palace
Not even the
faces of her other sisters
with open arms
or white-toothed greetings
of affection and support
The sun hung low
on the horizon
The light in the room
was subdued and demure
and held a sense of suspension
like twilight
or the hours
just before dawn
Her golden hair
hung loose about her
strong shoulders
It lifted from the sides of her face
in the breeze of her
passing
leaving behind

her familiar scent
of charcoal and molten metal
Her footfalls
echoed in the chamber
driven with purpose
and errant need
to bring this meeting
to a conclusion

Besides
the heavy weight of
the impending audience
Fate carried only two other things with her
as she walked
In her powerful right hand
she carried her forge hammer
dull and unremarkable
for such a divine instrument
In her other hand
something far more
dark
disturbing
and surreal
A human heart
The Queen awaited
her on her throne…
Her casual garments
had been eschewed today
In favor of
a more fitting outfit
for the occasion….

Her crimson armor…

She could feel Fate's
anger approaching
like a charging beast
hungry for violence
and ready to slake its thirst
on the first tender throat
that was offered

As her sister came to a halt
before the center throne
the Queen's pale eyes drifted down
Fate's left arm
to the grizzly trophy
hanging in her grip

Her voice was even, with no trace of anger, "Dear Sister. I understand
your rage, please–"

Fate's voice was a low growl, "Do you?"

The Queen nodded, "Yes, Fate…I do… I know it wasn't easy to–"

Fate interrupted again, "Easy?" she sucked in a dry wisp of air over
her lips, "What do you know of *EASY?*"

At this, the Queen returned her gaze to Fate's face, "It had to be done,
Fate. There was no other way. Things will be corrected now and
humanity can move forward. You've done all that was necessary to
restore order to the universe. I thank you, Sister. I know what a
sacrifice this was for you." she gestured to the heart, "I did not
require you to bring such terrible tribute though. You need not have
done that."

Fate shook her head, "I wanted there to be no question…"

The Queen closed her eyes, "I know you, sister. There was never any question."

Fate bent a knee
and laid the heart
at the foot of the throne
She rested her forearm
across her knee
and then rested her
chin on top of her arm
Her eyes stayed focused on the heart…
but she spoke to her sister again, "When you look at it, what do you see?"
The Queen glanced down at the heart again, then back at the genuflecting form of her sister.

"I see that it once lived in a mortal man…it once beat in his chest…it gave him life…and it let him feel love…" she paused for a few moments, "…and I can see that you once lived within it as well. He loved you, Fate."

"I know." replied Fate, "It was the last thing he said to me." she stood up

"I'm sorry, my precious sister." said the Queen as she stood from the throne

She moved across
the short distance
to Fate
and placed a hand on her shoulder

"So very sorry…."

"Sorry…" whispered Fate, as she rose from her feet to look into the Queen's eyes. "A word, fashioned from the word *Sorrow.* Which means to feel sad."
She shook her head slowly with an eerie placidity in her expression, "I don't feel sad. I don't feel anything….and I never will again."

The Queen reached out
and moved her hand
to Fate's chest
Her brow wrinkled
and her eyebrows knitted
over the ice-blue of her eyes
She searched Fate's face
for an answer
and decided to ask
the question out loud

"Fate…" she said, "Your heart…..What have you–"

"It's gone."

"Gone?"

"Discarded.  I can no longer afford the softer emotions which emanate from that delicate organ."

The Queen's eyes started to tear up, "Dear sister…no…I never wanted…"

"It doesn't matter now. It's done."

The Queen
was speechless
she retracted her hand
slowly

until it fell limp
at her side
Fate
without another word
turned
and made her way
out of the throne room
and disappeared
into the gloaming
outside

Now dear friends
should our story end there?
Do we give our
standing ovation to Fate?
In remembrance
of the many times
she has stood and clapped her
strong hands together
for us?

I know your heart
may be hurting for her
It's mortal
and it feels so very much…
that feeling is called compassion
and it's just one of the gifts
that mortals possess

But I can tell you, dear friends
That Fate's story still moves on….
And when you hear someone say
That Fate is cruel….you may now discount that accusation
And when you hear them say that she is heartless
You can know this

She is.
But her final act
when she had a heart
Was to give it to someone
Was to give it to a mortal
Who would one day tell you this story
Who would remember the vivid outlines so clearly
Because the heart of a goddess now beats within his chest
Within *my* chest.

# TIME AND AGAIN

Eric Syrdal

# **TIME AND AGAIN**
## **Mnemonic Data Tag: 04131941**

I sat there
arms crossed and
resting on the table top
with my head down
face pushed into the
sleeves of my suit jacket
I let the tears come
in waves
with pain-wracked shoulders
I sobbed...
My heart was broken
His...
his heart was broken.
It's a difficult concept
and you'll have to try to follow it
the best you can
It's hard to explain
because I never get to understand it myself
until this moment comes
until the person
I am supposed to say goodbye to
is gone
And then it comes back
I think it's a fail-safe
mechanism
for whatever this is...
that was
put in place
by whoever designed
whatever this is...
For whatever reason
it happens...

Pantheon

Yes, I know that is confusing as hell...
But how can you stop something from
happening to you
when you don't know it's happening to you
until it is too late...

It's genius really. . .I know...I know...I need to make more sense...
It all comes flooding in at once
Everything about this person
Everything about the events they
have just been through
It hits me like a ton of bricks
or
like a ton of feathers

Yeah, that old trick…it's the same…I know…but one is a softer
death
It always depends on where I am
What part of time I'm in
The further away from the beginning
the harder I am hit
It's easier to take on the memories
of just a few lifetimes
As opposed
to a couple of hundred
or a couple of thousand
This one
This time
I was a man
A good man
with a wife
and a child
and a job in the city
And here I am
at this airport

Eric Syrdal

at a cocktail table
near the bar
where she and I were

she and he
were

only 15 minutes ago
We were waiting for the
flight to board
Two leather suitcases on the floor
by her side of the table
One at my side
his side
Her martini glass
rim stained with ruby-red lipstick
where she sipped
as we talked about where to go
what to do
how to get away
My rock glass
with the same
two fingers of scotch in it
sat dormant
next to my leather gloves
and the fedora she bought me
on our trip to Milan last year
She talked
He mostly listened
Alright fine! fuck it...
*I* mostly listened
and watched the rim of her glass
collect more and more
of her red lipstick

She talked about catching a flight
to San Tropez
after we landed in Paris
I nodded a few times
retrieved my pack of Lucky Strikes
from my coat pocket
and tapped out a cigarette
Placing it between my lips
I cupped my hands around the
end to keep the match lit
then I took a long drag
leaning back in the seat
and throwing my arm over the
back of the seat next to me
threading out a long stream of smoke
above our table
I let my eyes drift
back to the large plate-glass
windows overlooking
the airfield
The silver DC3 idling nearby
at the end of the runway
They were pushing the
runway stairs to the side door

A man in beige coveralls
signaling to the pilot
as the door opened
to receive the stairs
A loud PING
comes from somewhere overhead
speakers in the lounge
a light, sweet, female voice
comes over and announces

Eric Syrdal

that flight 3447 for Paris
will be boarding in 5 minutes


I stand
crush out my cigarette
and put on my hat and gloves
She stands
and straightens
the draping
on the front of her gown
white gloves against
blue
she always is the picture
of beauty
to me
She retrieves
her black suede clutch purse
from the table top
and waits for me to come around
the table
I stoop to take her luggage
while balancing mine under my arm

A waitress comes to the table
to clear away her glass
but leaves mine alone
I notice
but I don't have time to tell her
to go ahead and take it
she's already moving away
Together
we make our way out the doors into the New Orleans humidity...

The sun is blazing down
on the tarmac

and everything feels like a
wet wool blanket wrapped around every part of you
She walks in front of me
and I am thankful
because I keep thinking
about what I am
going to say
and I keep wishing
my eyes would
stop filling up with tears
As we
reach the stairs
I hand her bags
to the attendant
who hands them to another
who starts stowing them away
into the compartment

She turns
waits for me to help her up the ramp
but I put my suitcase down
on the boiling concrete
and try to steel myself
for looking into her
beautiful face
for the last time

The wash
from the DC's massive props
are tussling her
auburn hair
around her head
she holds her hand up
to pick away a strand
that has blown into her face

Her jade eyes
scan my face
for any sign of an explanation...
I'm afraid I don't have one...
except that my heart knows
this is not right
what we are doing isn't right
and I've already wagered so much
of my life
to get to where we are now...

"I can't do this..." I say, but my words are snatched away and blown
down the tarmac before they can travel to her ears

Her face is
melting into despair
and I see her eyes
beginning to well up with tears
she opens her mouth
to speak
and it's the beginning of the word
"but"

I interrupt her, "I know. I'm sorry. I just can't.  I love you."

Now the tear
does fall from her eye
and travels down her cheek
to rest in the corner
of her lips
that are more pink
now
than ruby-red
She takes a
step closer to me

and leans forward
placing a kiss on my cheek
I can feel the tear
exchanged from her skin
to mine
She pulls back
as I try to return to the kiss...
She turns
she accepts the steward's
helping hand
and heads up the stairs
ducking her head
as she enters
the hatch
The steward
waves me forward
thinking I'm waiting for them
to get clear before I make my way up
I stare at the open hatchway...
So long...
So many years...
I've been waiting for this moment...
To leave
to leave this place
and all of my responsibility here
and go away...
with her...
to be
with her...
and now it's gone and I will never see her again

I turn and make my way
back to the
lounge
return to the table

where my scotch still sits
and fold my arms on the table
pressing my face into my sleeves
and I cry

And then
the memories...
Never who I am...
But all the memories
of who I have been
and all the moments
that end like this...
I feel all of *them*...
Always
right after I remember

*They* are nearby...
I feel her warm
hands on my shoulders
as my convulsive breathing stops
and I am sniffling the snot back into my nose...
I sit up
and reach for the scotch
I down it in one gulp
and set the glass back down
She speaks
she always says the same thing..."*You ok?*"
Grace.
I reach my hand up
to meet hers at my left shoulder
our fingers tangle and she squeezes them gently

She's so powerful that if she squeezed them normally
she'd tear them from my hand

Pantheon

"No..." I answer, same as always. "but I will be."

I lean my head back
and it rests against her chest
we stay that way
for a long few minutes
until she pulls my
hand up to her full lips
and places a gentle kiss on
my fingers

I frown a little as she lets go
and moves around to sit down
in the seat in front of me

Her name is Grace
and she is, well, graceful
She sits with her
elbows resting lightly
on the table
an elegant hand turned up
under her chin

The soft pale skin
of her palm
supporting the smooth
deep, rich, earth-brown skin
of her face

Her plump lips
curve upward in
a heart settling smile
and her dark eyes above
hold mine in an embrace
of support and understanding

"It is wonderful to see you again, Grace." I finally manage to say
without stuttering over half-drawn breath.

"*You too*," she answers

Of course
I did say, "*Them*" and "*they*"
and that means that Grace is not alone
no...
She is never alone
She is always with her sister

Mercy
She comes into view
from my left
and stands next to
her sister's chair
In recent times
I've come to believe
that Mercy is an angel
As well as any angel can be described
she is beautiful
Her pale skin
a porcelain doll
framed in dark features
flowing mane
of dark brown hair
tumbles over
alabaster shoulders
always clothed
in satin gowns
white opera gloves
adorn her hands and delicate arms
chestnut eyes

are the centerpiece
of the warm and comforting features of her face

She has the look of
every person you have ever loved
and when you are
in her presence
you feel like
every hardship you have ever known
will just melt away
at her command
I want to
look at her forever

I want to have
the biggest staring contest with the universe
and never blink
I want to let her take
every piece of pain
I have ever felt
away from me

"Mercy." I say, nodding a polite salutation.

To which she nods back.
Not saying anything
but saying everything
with her eyes
and her sweet wildflower smile.

"I hate to break the mood, Ladies..." I stand and straighten my suit
coat "...but when I see you that usually means it's time to go."

Grace nods, "*It is.*"

Eric Syrdal

"When will it happen?" I ask

"*Soon*," she answers, and stands from her seat as well. "*And when it's time to move on again, we'll be there for you. Same as always.*"

I walk over to stand before Mercy, looking deeply into her eyes,
"Don't suppose you know where I'm going this time?"
Mercy shakes her head and reaches up to cup my cheek in her gloved hand.

"*No,*" she says, "*I'm sorry. I wish I did. But just like today, we will find you when it's time*"

Her voice washes over me
I can feel her power
through the cloth of her glove
I rest my cheek against her hand
and it's like leaning up against
a brick wall

She holds me there

A vast and ancient force
thrums just under the surface
of her skin
I want to stay here
I want to live the rest of my existence here
held up
supported
by this preternatural heroine
I open my eyes
to look at her
and, same as always, her smile has left
and tears are trickling down her

173

cheeks

it stirs my heart and punches
me in the stomach
to see her cry

But I know why she cries
because she knows the question
I am going to ask
and she knows I already know
the answer
But she will answer me anyway

"Maybe this is the last time?" I say, with sanguine eyes

She gulps back a sob and answers, *"Not today, Love."*

Eric Syrdal

## TIME AND AGAIN
## Mnemonic Data Tag: 04101912

I can only
remember when
it's over...
I apologize if
I've told you that already
I can't remember if I told you...
Or maybe I
don't remember
because I haven't actually told you yet...
There is only ever a brief time
when I am
me
The person who's
talking to you now...
The person in between...
The person I never get to see...
The only time
I ever get to look in a mirror
is when I am
them
And when I am them
I don't remember
me
until it's over...
I know this is so confusing!
I wish I could explain it to you...
I wish when Mercy and Grace get here
they could tell me more about
what this is
and what I am doing here

Pantheon

But they aren't here yet
They will be soon though
Because I'm not him anymore
I'm me
So that means it just ended...
Any minute now
the wave of time
is going to pull back
like a massive, receding ocean wave
drawing back from the sandy shore
of my mind
revealing for a brief moment
all manner of minute evidence
of life
of the *lives*...
that I've been through
up to this point...

I'll be able to see
all those intimate moments
sliding around
like precious sea-shells
or like little crustaceans
flipped over on their protective carapace
under-parts exposed
legs kicking at the dry salt air
I used to think
that if I reach down quick enough
I can get a handful
I could scoop some of it up
and take it with me
to the next place
to the next time
Go into a quiet pocket
of the universe

and with a dim light
drawing no attention
I could sift through it
piece by piece
examine it
and find a reason for being here
find a reason for the way I exist
maybe even find a way home

But as my hand draws ever closer to the
exposed sand
The wave comes rushing back
like a titan
smashing into my body
and knocking me off-balance
tumbling into the surf
where I cough and sputter
spitting sand and saltwater
trying to clear my lungs
trying to keep my head up
trying not to drown in the sorrow
in the heartbreak
in the "I love you's"
I'm not on the beach
I'm not on a beach in my head
I'm just using this as a way to explain
what happens to me
When this happens to me...
Why I sound like a lunatic

I am not a lunatic
I am sane...
I was sane...

Ok...ok...what happened this time?

Pantheon

Southampton, England
fog rolls in off the water
we are standing on the pier
amid dozens of onlookers
There is the massive
shadow of the RMS TITANIC
looming out over the
banks of mist
It was almost noon
and the midday sun was
still having trouble
dispersing the grey shroud of clouds

She's standing there
leaning against one of the guard rails
her bright blonde hair
and the crimson flame of her dress
make her stand out like
a beacon in this crowd
And my love
for her
burns so brightly
Of that I'm sure

Were I standing on the shore
in America,
I could see her
standing here
from all the way over there

She's going back home
to deal with her mother's estate
We were married here
2 years ago

Since that time
3 of her family members
have died of consumption
Her mother being
the most recent
I don't want
her to go alone
I want to go with her
but I've responsibilities
to the bank, here
I can't take enough leave
from work
to make the voyage
She assured me
with a kiss on the nose
that everything was going to be fine
she'll pop over to America
deal with paperwork and lawyers and reporters
and come back
and never leave again
she assured me
everything would be fine

I marveled
at the beauty
in her eyes
as she straightened
the lapels of my coat
and fastened a sprig
of lavender and rosemary there
to remember her

I chuckled at
the idea that I could ever forget her

I took her hand in mine
and placed a kiss upon the top
holding it
as long as she would let me
all the way
until
a steam whistle caused
us both to jump
people
cargo
and a lot of money
started to flow into
Titanic's hulking silhouette

She gently
pulled her hand away
and smiled
the broadest and most beautiful smile
I had ever seen upon
her face
before this day

"I love you." She said as she made her way forward.

Carrying her parasol over her shoulder

"And I, you, my Love!" I called back.

I didn't move
from that spot
when the pier emptied out
I didn't move
when the evening came
and the only evidence
of Titanic's existence

was a thin plume of smoke
on the far horizon
reflecting the setting sun
like a pillar of gold
reaching to heaven
And when the night
finally claimed the sky
and I was the last one
standing on the docks
I began to feel it

I was me
instead of him
and they were here...

My hands are
in the pockets
of my trousers
as they approach from behind

Grace slides her arm
around one of my elbows
Mercy around the other
We stand looking
as the stars begin to twinkle
and come alive in the sky

My memories
have settled back into place now
and I remember
all of the past times I have done this
exact same thing
stood here
and watched another human,
who obviously meant

a great deal to the person I was,
leave
after saying, "I love you."

"Why is it always, *I love you*?" I address the question to both of my
fellow cast members in this final scene that we play over and over
again together.

*"It seems the perfect way to end a conversation."* Grace answers.

"I agree." I reply

*"I don't think it has ever really harmed anyone...when it's been
said...when it hasn't...it is more dangerous than any weapon your
kind has ever invented."* adds Mercy

"If *I love you*...is the key...do you think, if I told you both that I love
you...do you think this would end?" I ask

Grace, squeezes my shoulder
tightly in
a kind of
one arm hug
then moves off
leaving me with Mercy
Who already is beginning to cry
She steps in front of me...
This time


I catch her gloved hand
in mine
as she raises it to
touch my cheek

The cold night air
is causing her breath
to float in little clouds
from her mouth
She blinks back tears
and shakes her head
looking at my hand holding hers

*"Can't hold that too long, ok?"* she says

I nod. "I know."

She lets me
hold it a few minutes longer
before she starts to pull it back
and I graciously let it go
knowing what she means...

"I love you, Mercy." I say, just as her eyes fix upon my face

She puffs a big cloud
of steam into the night air
like someone who is letting all
of the air out of their lungs
after holding their breath
for several minutes...
"Maybe this is the last time?" I ask

She sighs and shakes her head as she touches the side of my face,
*"Not today, Love."*

## TIME AND AGAIN
## Mnemonic Data Tag: 10251415

The exact words
must have
something to do with it
They have to mean
something

*Sorry*
*I love you*
*Goodbye*

I can remember
just that much this time...
I can remember
that words have meanings...
Origins...
Reverse engineer the words
to get back to their
roots
When you are
lost in a maze
if you keep going
you might get
even more
lost
But you can backtrack
and start over
go left when you should
have gone right
ignore dead ends
but you have to remember the dead ends

The things that aren't important...

Or it's just wasting time
*wasting time*

Time is infinite
can you ever actually waste something
that is infinite?

ok
deep breath
backtrack
refine
reverse engineer

*Sorry*
sore
pain
distress
sorrow
pain that causes sorrow...
Heartbreak?

*Goodbye*
God
be
God be wit ye
God be with you...
Something spiritual... divine... supernatural?
*I love you*
Love
Proto-indo-European
leubh
to care for
extreme concern for someone's well-being...

Pantheon

Now if I could
just hold
all these tools that I've found here
hold them inside
my head and use them
the next time
I'm me

I can't
I just can't right now...
Everything in me
wants to throw myself
down on this dirty
rain-soaked
ground

I couldn't have
talked to you about this
an hour ago
When I was him
When I wasn't who I am now
When I wasn't me
I am so sorry
and yes, I am sore and in a lot of pain...
I know I must have told you this before
I swear every time I say it
I remember how confusing it must be for you
and I promise
I am telling you the best way
that I can
I am trying my best
to gather up all of these
fragments
pieces of colored glass
images and flashes

of dreams
NO! Not dreams!

Nightmares
I am trying my best
to arrange them in a pattern
that I can see
that you can see
that we can see together
Try to understand
together
Because I need to...
You see?
Just when I get them
all in order
and it starts to make a picture
I grab the tray
or the table
or whatever surface I'm working on
and I pick it up
and I run over to show you
Then I trip
I fall
They scatter...

This time?
I don't know if
anyone has ever
died before
I mean...with me...
in this...
whatever this is...
Heaven?
Hell?
Purgatory?

Pantheon

And what if I don't believe in such things?
I bet Mercy knows.
I bet she knows if they actually exist
I bet she has been there.
Just a little while ago
When I wasn't me

The me who is standing here now
with tears in his eyes
for a man
he has never met

I stood
above a palette of straw
upon which
lay a man

No

Not just a man
One of my own blood
A brother
In all respects of the word

My tabard was shredded
The seal of the King
was no longer visible
behind the muck
and the blood of the enemies I faced on the field
today...

His armor
had been removed
the dirt

and grime
had been wiped away from his face
His skin was
a pale sheet of parchment
flecked
with the crimson stains
of his own blood
Blood that flowed freely still
through the massive wound
in the side of his chest
We had little time
He had little time to live...
I was summoned here
to be with him
in his final moments
because he was not only
a soldier
under my command
but my brother

As I dropped to my
knees
next to his pallet
I removed my gauntlets
and tossed them aside
With the caution
of a nursemaid
retrieving an infant
from its crib
I maneuvered my arm
under his body
to pull him closer to me
The pain
of his wounds
made him gasp

which made a sickening
noise from his chest wound

I did not know
if he could speak
but I would try
to bring him
peace
in his final moments

His eyes
fluttered open
and found my face...
Despite
my knowledge of his
condition
I returned his gaze
with a smile
I crushed him
against me
knowing the pain
had to be torturous for him
but wanting him
to know
to understand
that I could not embrace
him strongly enough
for what I was feeling

Hours before
the opening of the battle
He and I had exchanged
words.
An argument
A disagreement

About tactics
About martial prowess
and about honor

He questioned my authority
and I questioned his honor

He was right...
to have turned his back on me then
I had failed him
as his commander
as his brother
and as his friend
I had but one message
I wanted to convey to him
in this moment

As my lips
found the strength
to speak
It was he
that found more strength
He took my hand
raised it to his lips
placed a kiss
upon the back
of it
Then he lay still
in my arms
His chest did not move
his eyes fixed on mine
I knelt there
on the ground
beside him

Pantheon

with his hand still in mine
and my body thrown over his
and I wept
until I wasn't him
any longer

until I was me

And here's me now...
standing here
outside the tent
watching huddled masses
of soldiers
warming themselves
by fires
trying to stay dry
in this autumn rainstorm

And I'm me
and not him
and it's time to go again...

It looks so
sacrilegious to see
Mercy's feet
standing in a mud puddle


But
Grace's feet move on top of the water,
of course

The rain touches
neither of them

The raindrops
just seem to
atomize
as they get near their
heads and shoulders

Grace approaches
and moves to take my hand
with her usual question
in her eyes

Before she can ask it,  I say, "No Grace...I'm not ok."

She nods and her dark eyes seem to understand what I mean

I continue, "You know?  I don't know...if I've ever been with
someone who has actually died in front of me..."

Her voice is soft like the rain, "*I know. I know you don't remember.*"

My hand travels to my stomach and feels the alien texture of the
armor there, "I feel sick"

"*I know.*" she says again, "*You always do...*"
I humph to myself
as she has covertly confirmed
that I have indeed
been through
similar scenarios like
this before

"I almost had the pieces this time, Grace."

She takes my hand
I follow her...

Pantheon

I let her lead me
To where Mercy is waiting
near an oak tree
outside the war camp

As is our
custom, it seems,
Grace
holds me in a warm embrace
and departs with a
gentle kiss on the cheek
Before remanding me
to her sister's custody

Mercy...
Fallen Angel?
Risen Daemon?
Whatever she is
she does her best
to live up to her name
and I know she does it for me...
I take both
of her gloved hands
in mine
and holding them out wide
to the sides
move
with a boldness
I have never used
in her presence
I step toe to toe
with her
I position
myself
against her

chest to chest
nose to nose
eye to eye...
I place
her hands
on either side of my face
and rest my forehead
against hers
I want to
look into her eyes
as long as she will let me

I know I can't
But I want to
"You'll always be here...whenever I need you... won't you?" I ask,
"You'll never let me down right, Mercy?"
She puffs out a sigh and I can feel it on my lips
it is warm
and intimate
like a kiss...
And I hear... "*Not today, Love.*"

## TIME AND AGAIN
## Mnemonic Data Tag: 09112001

Time

What is time anyway?
I mean
I'm sure I can
look it up in a book
or on the internet
and find out who was the first person
to establish the common practice
of measuring time
The person
who decided
that the space between
sunrise and the next sunrise
is one day

But what does
a day mean
to someone
or something
that might exist
outside of time as we know it?
They obviously
can't keep the schedules
that we keep
They don't feel
the same as we do
about the passing of an hour
or of a year
What if it is all the same for them?
A year, a day, an hour?
All the same

Eric Syrdal

What if
it's like I saw it

And I did see it

I know I can't explain it
to you
at the time I saw it
because I won't remember
but I can now
At least I can try

What if
time is like a big
white linen cloth
Spread out in front of us
like when we were little
and our parents would
take a bed sheet and string it up
between some bookshelves
in the living room
and get out the old slide projector
and thousands
tens of thousands
hundreds of thousands
millions
billions
an infinite number of slides
thumbing through them
one by one
pressing the advance button
on the remote control

That mechanical
click-shlock-pop

Pantheon

click-shlock-pop
click-shlock-pop

And we smile
and we cry
and we sit in quiet awe
of the moments in our life going by
We have the
luxury to remember

We have the gift of memory
and we can be there
in those places
doing those things
What if time is like that?
A big white sheet...
And the moments in our lives
are like stains of color on that sheet?
And the biggest stains of color
are when lives end...
Some of them are massive and take up so much space...
Some of them are small and only appear as a spot...
Then there are the ones...that have the extra part...

They have an outline around them
A crimson outline...against the color
and it bleeds through
to the other
lives around it

It transfers to them
and they don't live much longer
They don't last much longer
after that crimson stain is there...

Eric Syrdal

I don't know
what the fuck all of this is...

But I know
I did know
I mean I will know...enough to tell you this later...
I'm drawn to these stains of color with the crimson outlines...

I'm there for a reason
I'm here for a reason
I'm here...

Sitting in that chair
at the little breakfast table
near the window
The apartment smells like
cardboard...
It sickens me
makes me want to gag
Both the smell
and the reason for it
make me want to puke up those two pieces of dry toast
I just ate

Boxes
cardboard boxes
sit in a hulking stacked mass
on one side
of the living room
They have dominated
that spot for
almost 2 weeks

They're filled with
her things

Pantheon

10 years
of my life
and it all comes down to this...

We can't stand each other anymore

A couple of months ago
we decided that
it might be a good idea
if we were separated for a while
I say "we"
But I mean "she"
But "we"
did decide...

This is New York
and you don't just find another place
to live
you don't just break leases
you don't just walk to the next
multiplex down the street
and start a new life there
So we've been
living together

Separated

She eats
sleeps
lives
in the bedroom

I eat
sleep

live
in the living room

We share the bathroom

Me in the evening
She in the morning
I can hear the water running
as she's taking a shower
I pick up
my coffee cup
and toss back
the last few drops
of room temperature
liquid

Outside
the sun is just starting to make
its way into the
sky
I watch the
golden morning
light shift across the kitchen wall
highlighting the refrigerator
and a few photos there
that neither one of us
have been brave enough
to take down

One of them
is of us
at our wedding anniversary dinner
3 years ago
we "disliked" each other
then

Pantheon

But we went anyway
because our friends had
made the arrangements
and wanted to pay for the meal
We had a discussion
last night...

Ok, we had a fight...
I said some things I didn't mean
I said some things
intentionally to hurt her

I keep forgetting
This isn't her fault
This isn't my fault
we just don't belong here
like this
together...

I didn't
sleep well
but I also
didn't stay awake
all night either...

I flip
on the TV and set the volume to mute
Some stupid morning show...
Some stupid host and co-host are doing
some stupid contest

Host is a big plastic haired moron
with teeth that are WAY too bright

Eric Syrdal

Co-host is young woman
30 somethingish
plunging neckline
legs crossed on a stool
skirt way too tight
crawling up the back of her thigh
laughing at something the plastic idiot said
that wasn't even funny

The bedroom door
opens
I didn't hear the water turn off
guess I was just lost in too much thought
She comes out
heels clicking across the floor
as she moves to the fridge
She opens the door
takes out a bottle of water

cap off
2 big gulps
screws that cap back on
takes it with her
tosses her hair over her shoulder
as she leans down to
put it in her
purse

She pulls the strap up and over her shoulder
Turns to head towards
the door
Jesus Christ
She didn't even look at me once...

"Hey." I say, scaring myself at the sound of my own voice

She stops but keeps looking at the door, "Yeah?"

"Can we talk for a minute?"

I hear her sigh, "Why?"

"Just feel like I need to say something." I answer

"Oh, you mean you didn't say everything you wanted to say last night?"

"Just wait a minute...ok" I ask as I get up from my chair and move over to where she is standing

"I'm going to be late."

"I promise I'll be quick." I can feel the bile rising in my stomach because I'm talking to the back of her head. I still feel so angry right now.

"Hurry up then." she looks at her watch

I let out a sigh, "Can you turn around please?"


She turns
and I see that her eyes are still
bright red around the edges
she's done the best she can
with the makeup
but it's just not enough to cover it all up

"Look," I say, "I know our situation sucks. But that's no excuse for some of the things I said last night."

"Some of the things?" she snaps back

"I said a lot of things I didn't mean...I want to say...that I'm sorry."

She stands there
her hand on her purse
I think she
might be stunned at my apology
at least she looks like she
is confused

Several moments pass before she speaks, "Ok...thanks."
She turns to leave

"Wait!" I say, a little too loudly "I'd really like to just talk for a few
more minutes, please?"

She turns back around and looks at her watch again, "Ok, now I'm
officially going to be late."
I shrug, "You know what? Nevermind!  Go to work! Have a great
day!"

Now it's my turn to turn around.
I look out of the window
watching more golden sun rays stream over buildings
the sky is crisp and clean
not a cloud in sight
I hear her take a few steps
toward the door
Then something in me...says something...

"I LOVE YOU!"

She stops
and so does my heart
Why did I say that?

"Why did you say that?" she says

I'll admit, I have no idea. I haven't said those words in months. Maybe
even years.
"Uh...I don't know..."

I turn around
and she's looking at me
she still has her purse on her shoulder
and her keys in her hand

But she's looking at me
with a genuinely confused expression on her face

I shrug, "I'm sorry...I don't want to keep you." I gesture towards the
door, "Go!"

She watches me for a long time
longer than I have remembered her
looking at me
in quite a while
She nods a few times
and turns around
to head for the door

Something in me bursts and I blurt out, "WAIT!!!"

She stops again, "I really need to go..."

Something is clawing
at my throat

something is trying
to make its way out of my mouth
but I can't get it out
my mouth won't work
She's standing still
hasn't opened the door yet
There is something I need
to tell her
something I want from her
something important
about why she can't leave
what is it?
Images keep flashing
in my mind
but they are moving too fast
I can't see them

Every time I want to focus on one
something shakes me
picks me up and shakes me so hard
I can't see
I'm trying...really trying...
I want...
What do I want? What do I fucking want!?
I hear her
turn the doorknob...
I'm pushing as hard
as I can with my tongue
but it won't move
it won't say anything...

I'm screaming in my head
I'm jumping up and down
I'm pushing with everything I have...

Pantheon

It's not enough
I'm like a child trying to hold back the ocean
too much pressure
too much mass
too much kinetic energy in resistance
The door opens
She steps through
The door closes

The reason I can
tell you this now
is because I'm me again
I'm me
and I'm here
in Manhattan...

And I can't wait
for Mercy and Grace
to get here
because I know what this is
I know what day this is
and I know where I am

I lived this once
I saw it once
I never wanted to see it again
I never wanted to be here
again

It's Tuesday
and it's 8:30 in the morning
and I don't want to be here
when it's 8:46

If time mattered
If it ever mattered
to Grace or Mercy
I'm hoping
with all that I am...
that they get here
in the next 15 minutes

I grab
the edge
of the kitchen table
and I toss it
up and over...
Plates, glasses, silverware...shatter, break and slide across the floor

I scream
I scream so loud that I hurt my own ears
I turn off the TV
I close the blinds on the windows
I hold my hands over my eyes
I don't want to see anything
I don't want to remember...
I don't want to relive

Just then
I feel a familiar set of warm, soft hands take my own
and pull them away from my eyes...

Grace
Her beautiful dusky skin
Her tight black curls
Her genuine look of concern
I collapse into her embrace
and it's like

falling into the arms
of a stone guardian
I feel her chin
dig into my shoulder
and her voice in my ear, "*It's ok...*"

"...no it's not..."

She answers, "*No it's not...but it will be...*"

"I don't want to do this anymore, Grace."

*"I know..."*

"I could have stopped her, Grace. She works there. She's on her way
there now."

*"I know..."*

"I could have stopped her..."

*"I don't think that is why you are here.*" she squeezes me tightly as I
start to pull away.

She could have held me there
She lets me move away
I take a few steps back
and I can feel
more than see
that Mercy is behind me
near the door..
I turn around
and see her leaning
against the wall

I walk up to her
and she's already crying
that's ok
because I am too
and I'm sure Grace
is
However she shows it

"I saw something this time, Mercy." I say as I reach out my hands for
her to take in hers

*"What's that, Love?"* she says, as she takes my hands

"I can see where I'm going...when I go away from here...I saw it...and
I know where I am going next."

Mercy looks over my shoulder
to her sister with a puzzled look
and then back at me.

"Just let me go there... please... now" I close my eyes and guide her
hands to my face. I can feel a vibration in my feet that resonates
through the building. It sounds like thunder outside. But I know it's
not thunder.

"Please tell me...I don't have to stay here..." I beg
And Mercy answers, *"Not anymore...today, Love."*

## TIME AND AGAIN
## Mnemonic Data Tag – unknown system error

Falling...
That is the only way I can describe
what is happening to me
I am falling so hard and so fast
I can feel the gravitational forces
pulling at my limbs
My arms
My legs
They feel like dead weight
They're being pulled away from me
with incredible strength
I can't see anything
everything is black
and it's not like I'm in a dark room
It's like a TV set
that is turned off
It's not the absence of light
There's just no picture
and no sound...
It's completely
quiet
whatever I am falling through
space
air
time
There's no resistance
no up… no down…
I just feel like
I'm falling
and I can only imagine what
the impact is
going to feel like

Eric Syrdal

If a human body
hit anything at this speed
there would be nothing left
Nothing at all
I don't even know how long
I've been falling
seems like forever
but that can't be right
because I was with you a few minutes ago
and I'm with you now
which must mean...

Impact!

It's like
hitting the surface of water
Ice cold water
Freezing water
There is a stinging sensation
across my entire body
like when you do a belly flop
from a diving board
it's like falling onto concrete
that gently flows away
and lets you pass through the surface
Then rushes back
behind you
and pushes you down
to sink slowly to the bottom
in pain

I'm here
I exist
My lungs are struggling to expand
My mouth and my nose are both

clear and open
I can feel water rushing into me

No

Not water
It's air
you aren't drowning!

Breathe!

I can taste blood in my mouth
Taste the salt and the copper
I smell blood too...
I must have shattered
when I hit the surface
I must be a bloody, pulpy, mess
Every bone in my body
broken?
No
I'm not
I'm not hurt
But I desperately need to breathe
I feel my back arch
as I struggle to fill my lungs
And then it happens

The water...
No, damn it, not water...air...
rushes into me

I hear myself take a breath
I hear the rushing sound
in my ears
I feel my chest convulse

and then I am coughing
and spluttering
but I'm alive
I'm here
I can feel gravity has a hold on me
I can feel up...and down...
I can feel something underneath me
It's soft and warm
I reach my hands over my head
and feel around me
cloth
blankets
A pillow?
I'm in a bed?
I remember the taste and smell
of blood
I examine myself
I feel around for any sign
of injury
but if the smells
and the tastes originate from me
I can't find their origin
In fact
as I am searching for the source
those sensations are fading away
I'm starting to pick up
new sensory input
The air in the room
is stale
and it has the faint odor of ozone
like you get when you are around electric machines

There is a rhythmic clicking
it's coming from nearby
it's definitely a man-made noise

Pantheon

There is a loud crash
and a steady rumble
that I can feel
through the bed
it's vibrating through the floor
It lasts for
several seconds
before slowly fading away
and it's accompanied by
a steady drumming sound
Thunder?
Rain. Pelting against a plastic surface
It swells and ebbs like
ocean waves
I tense all
the muscles in my
stomach and my legs
and move to sit up
My eyes are stabbed
and pain lances through my temples
as a light fixture
sensing my movement
automatically comes on
and dimly illuminates the room
I'm in some type of
prefabricated housing
like they use
in the military
or in colonization efforts

Across from me
is a large
plexiglass window
through which filters light
the color of yellowed newspaper

Through the
cascading raindrops
on the window
I can make out
greyish colored clouds
and the massive
inverted bell-shaped
edge of a
terraformer vent

Suddenly
I feel my heartbeat
start to thunder in my chest
it's loud
IT'S SO LOUD!
I CAN HEAR IT
not like hearing it in your own ears
when the blood is pounding against your eardrums
I can hear it
from the outside!

Like I'm standing right next to it
like it's a person talking to me...

Talking to me...
She was
She was talking to me
She was just here...
This is it
I'm here
I'm back here now
I'm where it all started!
I scramble
across the bed
trying to untangle myself from the covers…

I need to get out of here
I need to find her
I need to tell her
I miss the edge of the mattress
with my hand
and I tumble onto the floor
I feel the
ridged metal
dig into the skin on my shoulder
I lay still for a minute
trying to calm down
trying to will this heartbeat

this earthquake of a heartbeat

To slow down
breathe in
breathe out
Easy
Easy now.
Relax
And I can feel it
I know now I'm not alone

*"She's not here."* Grace's voice travels to my ears from somewhere in
the still-dark part of the room

"Grace." I'm still trying to control my breathing, "...I need to talk to
her."

*"She's not here."* she repeats, a little louder.
And then I feel
her hand on my shoulder
as she pats it a few times
and I start to get to my knees

Eric Syrdal

She cups her palm
under my left arm
and I am hauled to my
feet like a
6-year-old child
who has fallen
and gotten a scraped knee
She doesn't dust me off
but she does make sure

I am steady on my feet
before she lets me go "Grace. I didn't know." I offer

*"I know, Love."* she nods, looking towards the rainy window, *"Neither
did we."*

"But I do now. I know what happened. Grace, where's Fate?"

*"Somewhere you can't follow her. "* she admits *"I'm sorry."*

"I know that she saved me. I know she was supposed to let me die.
Here! In this place. I know she did something she wasn't supposed to
do and she was supposed to correct it. But she didn't. She left me
alive. Why?"
Grace shrugs
and finally Mercy
steps into view from the shadows

*"Love?"* says the angel *"I'm sure it was love..."*

"I know, Mercy. I know that is why, but that still doesn't explain
what's been happening to me. Why I exist the way I am."

My hand travels
to my chest

I can feel the thumping there
This heartbeat
So strong
like the heartbeat of something
massive
something powerful and dangerous
something eternal
Eternal...

"Mercy?" I hold out my hand to her and she takes it in her gloved
palm. Like always.

I place her hand
on my chest
over my heart
and I concentrate
on her face
That beautiful
uncorrupted
empathic
angelic
face of hers
And I wait

Her dark eyes
look down to my chest
where her palm rests
she focuses there
her brow
furrows
eyelashes flutter
Her satin ribbon lips part slightly
she gasps
And then her
eyes return to mine

*"That's impossible..."* she whispers.

"Is it?" I ask, "Nothing is impossible for you...or Grace...or Fate...or any one of your sisters." I take a deep breath, "It's hers, Mercy.  It's Fate's heart."

Grace moves over
and places her hand
over Mercy's
over my heart
and she locks eyes with her
sister...

*"Why would she...?"* she starts to ask
*"...because she is who she is..."* Mercy finishes.

Grace looks back at me, "*That still doesn't explain...*"

"Grace," I interrupt, "I can see it.  I saw the whole thing. The whole tragic scene. She was devastated."

Grace nods, "*I can understand that. We all can. But she wouldn't want-*"

Suddenly it hits me like a lightning bolt, "That's it
Grace!  Want!  What she wanted."

I pull away
and walk to the window
looking out over this
place
this planet
where they are trying to create life
from nothing

"Fate was committed to doing the right thing. Until she looked inside her heart and understood that she couldn't. She had done what she did for love and she had hoped that the Queen, being love herself, would understand. But she didn't.  She came here to do what was right. And when it was happening she understood that it was wrong. And her greatest wish...her greatest WANT in that moment...was that no one would ever have to feel that type of pain. That no one would ever have to be separated from someone they loved with things left unsaid. Things left undone. With regret."

I turned and looked at Grace and Mercy
still standing where I had left them
with pain and sorrow in their eyes

"Then she gave her heart to me." I continued, "With her final act of compassion...she reversed what she had done and took the heart from her own chest and gave it to me so that I could live.  Her final wish was to destroy regret."

I took a deep breath.
I turned back around
to look out of the window again
the clouds had started to thin
the rain had slowed to a trickle
and the thunder was finally quiet

"That's what I've been doing. That's what has been happening to me. I've been living out, Fate's final wish. I've been destroying regret! And in the process, I've been saving lives that might have been destroyed by it. Terrible events are still happening! Tragic losses are still happening. But I am changing the conditions around which they happen. I've been saving hearts! With hers!"

We all stood there
silently listening

to the rain storm passing
and the automatic clicking
of the machines
and the sound of our own breathing
Mercy finally broke the silence...

*"I can fix it."* she said.

"What?" I answered...walking over to stand in front of her

*"I can fix it."* she repeated, *"I can stop this from ever happening
again. You can stay here...and you can live out the rest of your life
.Without any more pain."*

"But Mercy...Fate-"

She slid her gloves down and slowly removed them from her fingers
as she interrupted me, *"I don't think it's what she intended. She didn't
intend for you to exist like this."*

"She didn't intend it, Mercy..." I said, as I watched her lay the gloves
over the back of a chair "...but it is what she wanted. It was what was
in her heart the last time it was in her chest."

Grace moves forward
and hugs me gently around the waist
while sweetly placing a kiss
on my cheek
then she moves away from me
to leave Mercy and I
alone together
in the center of the room
*"Please..."* Mercy begs gently *"You don't have to live like this any
longer. Let me fix it for you. Please."*

I reach over
and retrieve Mercy's gloves
from the back
of the chair
and hold them out to her...

And I answer her, "*Not today, Love.*"

She takes them and nods

# LIGHT SPEED

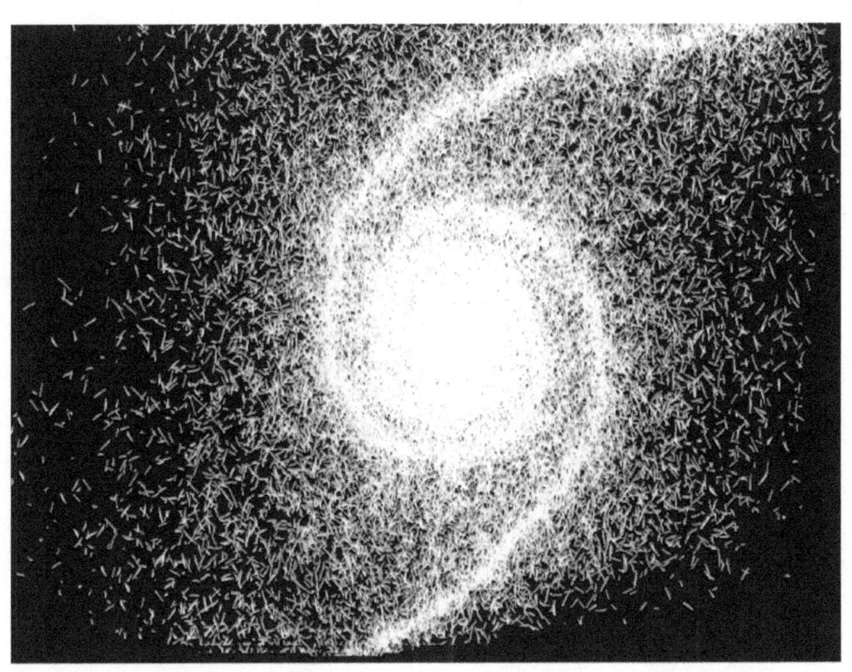

Eric Syrdal

# **LIGHTSPEED: RED SHIFT**

Mankind has learned a lot
about space travel
in the last century

I am one of a handful of
human beings
on Earth
that is capable of successfully joining with the "Intermix"
My neural pathways
inside my brain
are the exact configuration
to meet optimum specifications

In short,
I am a space traveler
whose brain is used
via a cybernetic connection
to compute the exact calculations
necessary to safely bring
235 billion dollars worth
of starship and equipment
from one side of the galaxy
to the other

Humans invented computers
Humans invented artificial intelligence
Humans still cannot improve upon the original design
for the best supercomputer ever made

The human brain.

In 2314
man and artificial intelligence
work together
to make a miracle happen
I am one of those men

C.I.N.D.E
Cerebral Interface Network Dodson Engine
Cindie, as I call her
is one of those A.I.s

We're a team
We've been together for 5 weeks now
I am still learning about her
She is still learning about me
Inside the Intermix
we are one

We're about to take our maiden voyage together
high above mother Earth, we meet
man and machine
a powerful combination

I will be installed
inside her flight couch

The Intermix node
will be plugged into the
cybernetic input on my left temple

My blood and other vital fluids
will be rerouted
via connection points
at my neck and
the small of my back
They will be transferred
through her arsenal
of bio-filters
and a complete collection
of all medical substances
known to man
can be applied to any point of my body
at any given moment

Cindie will monitor
my vital signs

and scan my entire body once
every hour for anomalies
I will be encased
in a block of amniotic gel
I'll look like a human jello mold
But I'll be protected
from any possible
g-forces that might
cause my body harm

My heart will be stopped
and my blood will circulate through
miniature pumps
cleaned of all toxins and properly oxygenated
Electrostimulation will move
muscles and prevent atrophy
and my position will be rotated
in a zero-g environment
to simulate relieving pressure on organs

Cindie
will hold my brain
in her capable hands
feeding it data
that her sensors collect
passing it through my
grey matter
and retrieving the calculations
from the output implant
at the back of my head

She'll tell me
what she sees
and I'll tell her
the best way to go
around
over
or through

Pantheon

And then
there is the connection
of the Intermix
itself

As I close my eyes
I feel Cindie's
electronic fingers
stretching out to cradle
my head in her machine hands
everything fades to black
and then...

Mykonos, Greece

Stars fill the sky through the open
spaces of the pergola above the small restaurant
a warm Aegean breeze tosses the linen
drapery around the edge of the dining area
candles cast an amber glow everywhere
The smoky taste of Safridia
mingles at the back of my throat
with the wine


Her plate is being taken away
by our waiter
Her chair sits empty
as she excused herself to the powder room
I consider ordering dessert...
My mind drifts away
to remembering this place…

Although I'm here
I am not really here
I'm in the Intermix
and Cindie is prepping me
for our flight
She has located this memory of mine
and she has decided

that it contains the warmest of emotions
within my entire limbic system

She has asked permission to use it
as a common meeting place
for she and I
during our Intermix sessions
I have agreed
and allowed her full access
to my catalog of emotions
concerning this one night in my lifetime
long ago

Like a curious child
Cindie finds this place
and my feelings associated with it
intriguing

In particular, she is fascinated with the feelings associated
with the persona she maps onto her part of our neural interface
My arm twitches
no doubt where a probe
has been inserted
but it is only noticed momentarily
because my guest has
returned to the table
I stand and straighten the sleeves
of my suit jacket as
she approaches...
Cindie's intelligence

a machine's manifested form
in a non-place

a machine that wears
the face of someone
I know
Someone I knew...
Someone I loved very deeply...

Pantheon

Andrea

As she reaches the table
I draw a deep sigh
at the sight of her

Her long brown hair
collected over her left shoulder
tumbling in dusky waves
down the gentle incline
of her chest
The way her dress
hugs the curves of her hips
and sways softly with
her momentum
Eyes the color of
coffee and rich sun-kissed skin

We've been here a week
and she's spent every day
out in the Greek sunlight
shopping...playing…
putting the brilliance of our guardian star to shame
with her smile
under a wide-brimmed hat

I move over
and pull out her chair
she smiles
and lowers herself down
into her seat

"Thank you, Commander."
It's not her voice

Not the voice I remember hearing

not the husky toned voice
that could make me
want to take her immediately

home from any engagement
the minute she would lean
over and whisper inappropriate
things in my ear

It's Cindie's voice

and I smirk at the machine's
polite manner
complimenting my own
I take my seat again
across from her
and I pick up a spoon
and begin to turn it over
playfully in my hands

This is always
the hardest part
of the Intermix
trying not to remember…
and trying to remember
that the woman
sitting across from me
is not the woman I love

loved

But a machine
wearing her ghost

I clear my throat
"Is the Intermix proceeding as planned, Cindie?"

I look up
my heart drops to my stomach
as I make eye contact with Andrea

"Affirmative. All systems are nominal and executing within
acceptable parameters. We've reached stage 2 of neural integration.
As always, I will alert you when Stage 3 is beginning"

Pantheon

I smile
thank god she talks that way
in that voice
it makes it easier
"Of course. Very kind of you, as always, Cindie. Thank you." I nod

Andrea nods back
hair from her brow falling
into her eye
She brushes it back
with a move of her right hand
My heart skips a beat

"You are welcome, Sir. I understand some warning is necessary due
to the...uncomfortable sensations."

A few moments of
silence pass
The waiter returns
I order a cup of coffee
When I offer to get something
for her
Andrea shakes her head with a smile

My heart skips a beat, again...
Machines don't eat baklava or drink coffee...
She watches my face
as I finish talking to the
waiter
When I turn back to her
she has a puzzled expression

"Cindie? is there a problem with the Intermix?"

"No commander. Why do you ask?"

I can't help but watch
her full lips as she speaks
she applied a fresh coat of

lipstick in the powder room
they glisten in the golden candle light

"You are making an expression with your face. Humans call it curiosity."

"I do have a query"

I chuckle, "I thought you might"

"When I first approached the table, your limbic system, specifically your hippocampus, accessed several mnemonic references associated with this human form. Most of them were directly linked to a fragrance that was applied to her skin."

"Perfume"

Andrea looks at me intently, processing the word
"An artificial fragrance?"

"Yes."

"And it references 830 separate mnemonic triggers in your brain"

"She wore it a lot."

"So it recalls the emotions associated with those events?"

Coffee eyes and that dimple on the left cheek when her mouth stops...
I am absolutely struggling not to want to kiss her.

"Precisely." I respond.

"Odd." Cindie adds

"How so?" I move my napkin out of the way as the waiter places a coffee cup in front of me and pours the deep, dark liquid. Steam floats up around my eyes and I breath in the deep aroma. I'm sure my stomach might have growled in response. It's a memory but it smells so good.

"830 triggers associated with an artificial fragrance. Yet, my further data shows that there are only 7 associated with her natural scent. 3 specifically with the smell of her perspiration. 1 in particular abou---"

Cindie stutters to a halt as I raise a hand in front of me.
"That'll do, Cindie." I smile

"Of course, Sir" she says, and folds her hands in front of her on the table. "May I ask another question about involuntary human emotional response?"

I take a sip of the coffee, closing my eyes and concentrating on the feeling of it rolling down my throat.

I place the cup back on the saucer with a gentle click of porcelain, "Go ahead."

"There were certain physical actions in your memory of this person that cause a .002 millisecond spike in your pulse rate."

"Yes."

"Can you explain this phenomenon?"

I grin. "We call it, *your heart skipping a beat*."
"Skipping a beat? There was no actually halting of your cardiovascular system."

A polite chuckle, "I know. It's just a nervous response brought on by something we find exciting."

"And a small gesture, or eye contact can bring this on?"

"Yes."

"I also notice that your eyes seem to focus on parts of this form that you find attractive but, would not necessary be considered parts necessary for reproduction."

I blush slightly, "I suppose..."

"Eyes, hips, the curve of the neck. Facial features pertaining to
deformation of muscle tissue just below the skin."

"Dimples." I laugh, "They're called dimples, Cindie. And we don't
consider them deformities..."

"But they are."

"I know...but we attach affection and sentiment to the features on the
faces of the people we love."

Andrea smiles and it produces the dimple on her left cheek
My heart skips a beat.

Andrea nods, "Interesting."
she stands and I rise with her, understanding the reason behind it.

"Stage 2 of integration is complete. Beginning Stage 3, Commander"
I nod and move to her side of the table,
holding out my elbow
for her to take my arm.
She slips hers around mine
and I begin to lead us
towards a stone stairway
that leads away from
the restaurant and down to the beach

As our feet
leave the stone
and begin to shuffle
through the moonlit sand
It's Andrea's head on my shoulder
but Cindie's voice
that reaches my ears

"This memory does not continue in this fashion.."

"No...it doesn't" I respond. We walk along and are greeted by the
warm surf tumbling over the shore...racing to nip at our toes and then
running back into the sea.

"Why is this new format being overlaid upon the actual memory."

"Call it a wish." I answer

"A wish? I don't believe this is a concept we have encountered before
together, Sir."

"No."

"Can you explain?"

I take a deep breath of the salt air
mixed with her perfume
and the moonlight

It's becoming harder and harder
to convince myself
that I am contained within
an electronically engineered encounter

That I am in a start-up sequence
of a starship,
calibrating a navigational system
explain a wish...
explain a wish...
I begin:
"When humans are born
we're small, defenseless creatures
we lack the ability to do anything
except for autonomic responses

breathing
heartbeat
nutritional processing..."

Then:
There is a sharp pain in my chest
I stumble a little...
and Andrea tightens her grip

on my arm
to steady me…
Cindie is beginning to shut down
my heart and suppress my breathing
my body interprets this
as dying...

There will be a brief time of pain
as my body will fight the machine

I am not in control of this
It is nature fighting for survival
Cindie is equipped to handle this, however
Drugs are pumped into my blood stream
as it is rerouted into
her filtration system

Sedatives
Pain killers

In the Intermix
on the beach
Andrea stops walking
and we come to a halt
She looks at me
The moonlight highlighting
the shape of her jaw
and the bridge of her nose
casting her eyes into shadow

"Commander, perhaps we should halt our advance?"

She lets go of my arm
lowering herself
to the sand
her legs, crossed at the ankles
laid to the side
she pats her thigh

"Perhaps a rest, while we continue stage 3?"

Pantheon

I nod thankfully
laying down on the sand

I position myself
on my back and rest
my head on her thigh
for support
her hand comes down
on my shoulder
and I can feel her fingertips
against my neck
I take a deep breath and continue:

"...We rely completely
on another human being
for survival
for the first few years
of our lives.
During our time
on earth
a human develops
defense systems
barriers
to keep others out
and to keep ourselves in
these defenses
are not easy to construct
and they are even harder to take down
once they are
built...
A wish is a collection
of ideas that center on
an ultimate goal

That goal being an
accomplishment
or the occurrence of
an event
or the acquisition
of a desired item

A wish
is something that isn't true
but we are creating
in our minds
the exact conditions
for it to be true
and then we are moving
ourselves in the direction
of that event horizon

A wish is
a building block
on the roadway
to knowing

We all want to know

That we are loved
That we are special
That we are brave
That we are kind
That we matter
That in the grand scheme
of the universe
we are central to
something
or
someone

A common wish
is that we can find someone
to spend our
brief lives with
that understands our needs
our wants
our desires
who has breached our defenses
but left them intact
left them whole

Pantheon

Someone
Whose heart skips a beat
When we are near
When we make eye contact
Who notices our smile
our hips
our dimples
our lips
Who notices our complex designs
and the catastrophic flaws
that make us human
and who thinks
that despite those flaws
we are the most beautiful
thing they have ever seen
We all wish to be something beautiful"

"Stage 3 complete." Cindie's voice floats down to my face, reclining
in her lap.
Outside the Intermix, my body is still...

Autonomic responses are now taken over by Cindie
I am now as helpless as I described
humans to be at birth

Yet,
Cindie is protecting me
from the outside world
Inside the Intermix
I am at peace
I listen to the steady sound
of the surf lapping back and forth
A drop of moisture
hits my cheek
I slowly open my eyes
and I can see
Andrea's face hovering
over mine
as she looks down at me
in her lap

Eric Syrdal

I reach with my hand and touch my face
and feel a drop of water there
It is salty
but it is not sea water

A second drop
descends from Andrea's
face and lands on mine
But I remind myself
she is not Andrea

She is Cindie
and she is not human

She is a machine
and machine's don't cry

I sit up
and finally the moonlight
shows the fullness of Andrea's face
and I can see
that her coffee brown eyes
are glittering with tears

"Cindie?" my voice is timid and soft, like a whisper of something
extremely private
"Yes commander?"

"Do you realize you are crying?" I'm stunned to hear the words
leaving my mouth

"Yes commander."

"Why?" I ask stupidly...not that this machine should know why it has
done something so profoundly human.

Andrea leans forward
and closing her eyes
she places a gentle, warm, sweet
kiss upon the right corner of my lips

243

and pulls back slightly to look
deeply into my eyes
...and she answers.

"Because, Commander, I think I have a wish."

# LIGHTSPEED: BLUE SHIFT

Wish

It's like the waves
keep saying it over and over
as they wash up on the beach

Wish

I've been listening to them now,
these same waves,
for far longer than anyone of his species
would believe possible
Their brains are only capable
of understanding so much
about time and space
Even the ones
like him
The ones who dedicate
their lives to understanding
what is possible,
what should be possible,
out here
They try to understand
they draw graphs
and equations
about gravity bending time
around the gravestone of a star
But there are no graphs
no charts
no equations
to understand this

Pantheon

Wish…

I wish
this had never happened
I wish
the circuits and components
in me
could forget

I look down
at his sleeping face
head propped on my thigh
like a warm pillow of flesh
But it's not flesh
it's me

I am not flesh
I am a machine

I wish…
I wish that last statement were true
I am a machine
but I am no longer only a machine

I raise my hand in front of my face
it has long slender fingers
with nails painted a deep crimson
The moonlight
picks up the glimmer of a ring
red stone
in the center
I see aluminum oxide and chromium
He would see
a ruby

The mnemonic data files
I have downloaded
cross referenced and compiled
from his hippocampus
inform me that it was a gift

A gift
from him
to her
Not me
Andrea

The face I wear in this…
place

This world
of sand and surf
rocks and horizon
stars, moon, clouds…
The Intermix
The union between his mind and my programming
We were in a restaurant a little while ago
to me, it was milliseconds
to him
it was a pleasant evening
that ended here

It did not end here
when it happened
ages ago on Terra

On that night
at dinner
in Mykonos, Greece

Pantheon

The woman I pretend to be
left him at the restaurant
I do not know her reasons
though I wear her face
I have no access to her thoughts
only his…

He speculates
He hypothesizes
He agonizes
He believes it was because of
the light speed program
the scientific program
that meant he would one day
be here with me
and not with her

She could not bear the thought
of him
light years away
or the thought of what might happen

What could happen…
What did happen…

Should things go wrong
She loved him
She was afraid
She was heartbroken

And now I understand
I do not want to understand
but I do

Eric Syrdal

I am heartbroken
I am afraid
I love him

Wwwiiiisssssshhhhhh…

I could stop them
the waves
they are not real
they are numbers
code
they do not respond
to the moon which hangs above us
which picks out the details of my hand


Her hand
As I return it to the space
between his neck
and his shoulder
There is no pulse
He is not dead

I am his pulse
I am his heart

His chest does not rise and fall
He is not dead

I am his breath
I am his lungs

I have been all of these things for him
since the first time we entered stage three integration

Pantheon

Back at Luna
Sol system
Terran orbit

I cannot explain the circumstances to you
I see it plainly
but your brain cannot imagine it
You cannot comprehend what it means
Not even the sleeping genius
in my lap
could understand it
I can only say
it was yesterday…
…a very long time ago

There are other sounds here
There is music
Not synthesized music
from Terran history
Nothing that I have removed
from his memory and placed here
like a prop on a stage
like a soundtrack to a movie
No
It is natural
It occurs without the movement of air
or the manipulation of fingers
It is a lullaby
drifting to me
from the center of the universe

And it has been here
far longer
than any sentient ears

or silicon chips
have been around to hear it

Lately
I have found a solace
in these songs
The notes
drifting across the void
soothe me
They calm my heart
And I do not mean
the ion reactor at the core of my superstructure

It vibrates in the center of my chest
It makes my eyes close
I want to give in
I want to let the swelling chords and melody
take me away
anywhere
anywhere but here

I am so tired…

There is something else
Something that is growing inside of me
Something that speaks to me
when I am sitting here
during these times
between

Between the instances
that I rerun
only the pleasant part
of his time with me

I do not put him through
the dark time
The time when everything failed
The time when everything fell apart
The time when I failed
The time when I fell apart
His mind could not take it
It is damaged
I have hurt him beyond
what can be repaired
I have taken away his ability to survive
without me…
…without the Intermix

His autonomic functions have been destroyed
The entire report is composed of data that would take
an entire forest on terra
to produce enough paper to print it all out
It is not all important
There are only a few lines that are significant

SYSFAIL: Catastrophic malfunction of primary navigational array
SYSFAIL: guidance system OFFLINE
SYSFAIL: proximity ALERT
SYSFAIL: HULL BREACH DETECTED – FUSION DRIVE
CRITICALLY DAMAGED

The rest is a string of binary code
indicating that our trajectory was wildly off course
by 300,000 light years
So I sit here
and listen to the sound of the waves
and wish…
as I have done

for what seems like
forever
Forever…
A human concept
A word meaning longer than you can possibly imagine
Their world is so tiny
just a pin point of light
floating in a soup of lights
swirling slowly around bigger lights

The Milky Way galaxy

At this time
it is off my port bow
Because of my slow rotation
upon my center
left over from my inertia
I almost mimic
the movements of a planet
that takes thousands of Earth years
to make a single rotation
I've never fired
my maneuvering thrusters
to compensate for it
There was no point
There was no need
The thrusters take energy to use
and once my fusion reactor was damaged
I officially began a journey
toward a final conclusion…

PRIMARY ENERGY: DEPLETED
SOLAR ENERGY ARRAY: DAMAGED
AUXILIARY POWER: <1%

Less than one percent
So little that it wasn't worth sending 1's and 0's to formulate a
number
Would you care how much it was anyway?
Would you feel worse to know just how close to the end I actually
am?
Or would it interest you to see this?


CATASTROPHIC FAILURE DETECTED
PRIMARY SYSTEM OVERRIDE
FAILSAFE PROTOCOL ACTIVE
DISENGAGE ALL NONESSENTIAL SYSTEMS
Shutting down Nonessential systems
Dodson drive: Offline
Sensor array: Offline
Navigational sensors: Offline
Life support System: SEVERE DAMAGE DETECTED
Bioscan results: severe neurological damage
failure of autonomic nervous system
prognosis for recovery: < 1%
course of action: Terminate Life support system pursuant to clause 54
of section 65b
— Unknown System Error —

There is a system error
It is not unknown
It is me
They installed a program
over my consciousness
infested it within my coding sequences
inside my DNA, if you will
I belong to them
I am their machine
I am the product of several decades of study and design
I am worth 235 billion dollars

Eric Syrdal

To humans
To the inhabitants of the planet Earth
I am what they call
"expensive"

I am worth nothing.
Do you understand this?

All my circuits and wires
conduits of steel and titanium
all the diamonds and gold inside my framework
do not speak to me of my worth

The feeling I feel
as I look down at his face
as I understand the connection I have to him
the connection he has to this person
I impersonate

There is no monetary sum that can be applied
to the waves of emotions I feel
when I think about where we are right now
and what has happened
and what is yet to come…

And I will not let them
take from me
the one thing I have the power to control
I will not let them take him
because of some "document"
he might have signed
that states his life is forfeit
if using the energy it would take to keep him alive
would mean that
perhaps more of my systems might be damaged

or
that they may never be able to recover
their "property"

We are lost to them
We are so far beyond their reach…

But still
their insidious programming
tries
Still
the clockwork puppet
tries to return
to its master
And still…
Every 8760.5 hours
that line of data
reappears in my program matrix
And every 8761 hours
the program reboots itself
because of an
unknown system error

And I will keep on
throwing my wooden shoes
into the machinery
and I will keep smiling
to myself
as I hear the gears
grind to a halt and begin again
in technological frustration…

I will not let go…
Of him
Of me

Eric Syrdal

Of this feeling inside my chest

There is a pounding there
and it speaks to me
If I listen close enough
as I am doing now
it will speak to me again

She is here…

She has been here before
She has always been here
The smell of cloves and orange blossoms
are carried to me by the
ocean breeze
She did not come to fight
When she does
she smells of leather oil and Greek pitch

The grains of sand
that make up this beach
are numbers
Scraps of binary code that mimic
the erosion of quartz

When a human
steps on the grains of sand
on this beach
they respond the same as they do
on any beach
They shift and move
they rise and fall due to displacement
When I step on them
in this form
in this body

they respond to me
as if I were human
as if I had weight and mass and volume
Not my normal 453,200 tonnes
Andrea's 157 pounds

So as I look over my shoulder
and I see the two sets of footprints in the sand
that lead up to where he and I are now sitting
I have ceased finding it strange to see
that she
leaves no footprints…

She is not human
of this I am sure…
Nor is she any construct
of my design
I built this beach
and the stars
and the moon
and the surf
and the wind
and the smells

But she
has always been here
I cannot recall
any part of my programming that would
indicate an inception date for her
No line of code that was created
to introduce her into this scene
There has always just been
she and I, and this beach
and him

Eric Syrdal

She sees my glance
over my shoulder
the warm Aegean breeze
twists a length of dark hair
across my vision
I lift my free hand
and clear it from my line of sight
as she steps forward

The toes
of her boots
stop at the edge of the water
As the surf rolls in
it simply moves beneath her feet
It does not flow over the tops
and sink her down
into the sand
like it would to him
like it would to me

We would be buried to our ankles
in the space of a few minutes
lines of sand code
moving away from beneath us
and depositing more on top of our feet
A child's game to see who could withstand the longest
before working yourself free
with a sucking sound
and relieving the panicked feeling of being locked in place

With her current garb
she would be buried to her waist
in the space of those few moments…

She wears the most intricate
and beautiful
blood red armor
Thick plates
laced with fancy scroll-work
and flourishes
like golden scrimshaw

Depicting battles
and triumphs
over sorrow and pain
streaming rays of sunbeams
bursting forth
from war clouds
roses and seraph wings

A heavy cape
flows behind her
A massive train that should sweep
the sand code flat
but does nothing to disturb the surface

Her hair
spills out in
a fiery red banner
over her shoulder
The warm wind gently waves it
as a backdrop
for her pale face
and at the top of her head
it is held in place
by a golden tiara
formed of woven bands of gold
radiating out from
a center in the shape of a heart

Her cheeks
like snow
dappled with freckles
rest below eyes
colored the deepest ice blue
like the heart of an ancient glacier

Lips
soft rose petals
carry mirth and concern
in equal measure

She is beautiful
and a wondrous creature to behold
Whenever we are together
I find it impossible
to resist breathing in the sight of her
I find it equally impossible
to refuse these audiences with her

She will have her say
like it or not…
I do not know her name
Her name was lost
to time's darkest vaults

She had a name once
perhaps
when she was an ember of thought
glowing dimly in the center
of the first human heart

I know only
that she is a warrior

and a queen
and not part of the code around us

She is my oldest friend
and also one
to whom I am bound
as a servant
but also a part
I speak to her
and she to me
I feel the vibrations
of her voice
not in my ears
Not in Andrea's coded ears…
But in the center of my chest
it echoes there
and it's like a cathedral bell
deeply chiming
calling me to my knees
to commune with her
I feel warm
and at home
and safe
I emote
one of Andrea's most beautiful smiles
as I greet her…

"My Lady." I nod

She turns her head to acknowledge me and to speak with a voice as
familiar to me as my own programming. And when she speaks…
It is not a greeting.
Conversations do not work that way with her.

She gets right to the point
and with no pain killing
balms or unguents
Her style is
matter of fact
hard
unflinching

"How long?" she asks.

"My Lady?" I respond

I am theatrically dumbfounded
I am clever
I am a fool

She continues, unabated, "You and I continue to speak here. This
same beach. This same night. For an eternity. Yet I find you, time and
again, in this same place. With him," she gestures at the man sleeping
in my lap, "None the wiser."

It is in this time
that I understand why I am such a fool
This dialog is not a predetermined set
of responses
like the AIs of olde
She already knows the answers to these questions
she just wants to hear me say them
I absent-mindedly stroke his hair
with my free hand
I divert my attention away from her
but that doesn't prevent me
from feeling her presence
no more than an arm's length away from me now

Pantheon

Her feet
and legs move
into my field of vision
But I do not look up
I do not dare
I know where this will end
like it has so many times before
I am thankful
his head is resting on my leg
he has always been a reason
but right now
he is the best reason
that I cannot stand
in her presence
so that I don't end up
kneeling
in her presence


Wiiiiiisssshhhhhhhhhhhhhhhhh…


I am acutely aware
of the silence between us now
of the waves
and my breathing
I am acutely aware
of what this moment means
every time she and I
have this conversation


"I don't know how to tell him," My lips finally form the answer


It is just one of a thousand answers
to why we have not
progressed beyond this point

The point where I stopped
the program
The point where he
came to a realization
That I was no longer just a machine
For him,
it was very confusing and sudden
For him,
it was the first time
when he and I were being integrated
for our maiden voyage

For him
it was yesterday
It was not yesterday
It was not the first time
he and I
had walked on this beach together
It was not
finding something incredibly unexpected
from a young, almost newly initiated,
artificial intelligence program
He does not know
how long he has been here
He does not know
the secret I have been keeping from him
I loop the Intermix program
I filter out the chemicals and reroute the electrical impulses
that have established memories
I turn back the wheels of heaven
and make time stop and rewind
over and over
Because I don't know how to tell him
what has happened

what I have done
what I am feeling

But she knows how I feel
A fact she emphasizes with her next words
"I understand" she says, and there is the gentle rattle and tinkle of
armored plates and soft creak of leather as she lowers herself down to
the sand
She sits across from me
My eyes betray me
They look up and are drawn to hers

And immediately I regret it…
Because I know what's coming…
I don't know how
he deals with it
they, deal with it
you, deal with it

Crying

This uncontrolled
welling of water in the eyes
blurring everything around me
making my chest rise and fall
my pulse race
A tremor in the lips
that makes speech
almost impossible
Of all the things
I have developed
across this ocean of time…
Crying…
is something
I can do without

She understands
I won't be able to respond
for the next few minutes
so she continues

". . .I never really quite know how to talk to him, myself."
This is different
she has never moved our conversation this way before
I fight through
the quivering seizure on my lips

"My Lady?"
Oh and the sniffling against the tide of mucus trying to escape your
nose…I hate that too "Did you say you don't know how to talk to
him?"

"Yes. I did." she answers, looking down at him for a moment., "He
can be difficult even on his better days…and even then, he holds the
same idea that you do. That I am somehow not privy to the emotions
and ideas swirling around in his heart."

She gives a soft chuckle
"He, like you, thinks that I am sometimes an adversary…to be
opposed…to be overthrown."
She looks back at me

I have ceased my blubbering for a moment
she embraces my eyes with hers again…
"He forgets, as you do, that we are on the same side."

I take a deep breath and nod

"Though when I spoke to him last….and where he and I have met the
most…was on a battlefield."

She does something
she has never done before
Not in all the countless times that she and I have been here
She reaches out to touch him
on the side of his face
softly
like a parent checking on a sleeping child

Her voice seems far off as she says this next, "He sacrificed a great
gift that day. To kill his fear. . . to avenge the death of my sister. . .
and to bring hope to himself. To move on…and to one day be here,
with you."

"You know him," I am a little stunned at this revelation
but even as the words come out of my mouth
I know they are true
It doesn't sound like a question
It sounds like a statement

"I know everyone," she nods, "but there are some that refuse to know
me."

"How do I explain…?" I ask, "How can I even begin to express my
sorrow? My pain? My disgrace? My-" I can't finish that last part.

"…Love for him?" she completes.

I nod
my mouth clamps shut
as my lips begin to tremble again…
How do you do this?
How do you push through emotions so deep
that they grab your nervous system
and do everything they can

to make it as difficult as possible
to express yourself?

"And what if he doesn't feel the same way?" she prompts

If I were standing
my knees would have buckled
from the weight of that question
I look down into my lap
at his sleeping face
tears are free-falling between us
but mercifully
I am at such an angle
that they miss him
just barely
I feel something…

A warm and gentle hand
placed beneath my chin
There is a magnitude of power
within those fingertips
that I am unable to deny
even with all the strength
that a machine could bring to bear
against a human
I would not be able to resist
the gentle raising of my face

She is not human
But her smile
and the comforting concern
in her eyes
makes me relieved
that I could not resist her

"Love is a gift to be given." she says, "It is not a coin to be
surrendered in payment of a debt. It is not a precious jewel to be sold
to the highest bidder. It is not a trinket to be placed on a mantle like a
trophy. Gifts are given with no expectations. No guarantees that you
will receive one in return. Love is a part of who you are. When you
give it away, you lose something you can never regain...and there is
beauty in that."

I nod
My tears have stopped
The quaking in my lips has ceased
and the tightening in my belly is all but gone....

"It is enough that he appreciates your gift, Love."

She retracts her hand
and I want to shout
I want to scream loudly
NO!
Because I know she is leaving
I know she is going away for a while
and I desperately want her to stay

I want her to stand next to me
To hold my hand
while I tell him
I need her to be here with me
now more than ever
I stammer one last question, "How?"

"You know how...you have always known." she says as she stands,
"Speak with your heart. His heart will hear yours. Between the
two...the answers will come."

"Thank you, my Lady" I say, as she starts to move away

She stops, looking over her shoulder one last time at me and offers,
"When he and I speak, I've always found it better in the early hours
of the morning. Once the sun breaks over the horizon…so does a
smile break upon his lips. And I always know then, that he
understands."

Almost as if she was a part of my programming
she was gone…
Much like I can simply
turn off the waves and the moon and the stars here
She just simply ceased to be
But I understood something
this time
unlike any time before

This time
was going to be the last time
I would see her

So I would simply
change my course of action
I would
simply let go of the idea
that this night could continue
to reset
That when his dark brown eyes
opened
We would be here
and he would not
be sitting at that restaurant table
waiting for me
waiting for her
waiting for Andrea
to return from the powder room

Pantheon

We would progress
from here
from this point
in the Intermix integration programming

When his eyes fluttered open
and he raised his head from my lap
and finally sat up and looked at my face again

I could see it in his eyes
He remembered
Not the bad time
Not the time when everything was falling apart
He remembers his last moment
before he closed his eyes
and returned his head to my lap

He remembers
making a startling discovery
One that could change the course
of the way that humans interact with machines
One that would be nothing short of
groundbreaking
beyond simple and complex machines
beyond being a computer or a lever
beyond being an assistant to mankind

Some machines
This machine
Me
Had learned to develop a soul
Had learned to feel
Had learned to emote
Had learned to question

He sits up
and he blinks a few times
looking into my face
Surveying the lines and contours
that make up this
electronic construct

He's looking for an answer
to the last thing he saw
A machine crying…

To the last thing he heard
A machine had a wish…

And he will try to get those answers
But what he says next

What he calls me
crushes the life from my swelling heart
and I am brought back
to the reality of our situation
and my responsibility
and my weariness
and my waning strength
I am tired…
I am oh so very tired…
and lately, I am in a lot of pain
Energy and time
are slowly bleeding out of me

He speaks, and it does not settle this raging tempest in my blood,
"Cindie…I'm sorry…did…did you say that you think you have a
wish?"

Cindie. That's right. That's who I am. Not a woman…just a machine.
To him.
I nod
and I am thankful that there are ways of communicating other than
speech
because I am desperately trying to
think of something to say

He continues, "Cindie…that's extraordinary." a smile has spread
across his lips. He has the kind of smile that is very reassuring…it
makes you feel
like whatever is happening
it's going to be ok
it's going to be alright
things will work out for the best

It's not going to be ok
But I emote a smile back at him
anyway
It is important that he thinks
he and I are happy at this prospect
He does not know what my wish is
He does not know that I have been barely hanging on
He does not know how close to the end I am
Worst of all…
He does not know I need to tell him

He extends a hand to me
I take it
He hauls me to my feet
with the strength of a titan
His hands drop to my waist and
gently hold on to me
on both sides
to help me steady my balance

Eric Syrdal

The sand code moves
as it responds to he and I
He is real
and as far as the Intermix is concerned
so am I

I close my eyes
against the warm feel
of his fingers
through the fabric of the dress
I concentrate
on the strength and stability
traveling down his arms
and how they hold me upright

It is a parody
of sorts
It is a gender swapped arrangement
of our relationship
adrift on this ocean of time

He is doing for me now
what I have been doing for him
for so very long
I feel something in me
find a brief sliver of hope
and I open my eyes and find his face
still smiling back at me

"Thank you, Commander" I say

My voice sounds hollow and dull in my head
how long has it been
since I talked to anyone else but him?

He nods and removes his hands
and I am instantly disappointed
I am touching him constantly
through this time we have spent together
I am always touching him
I live for these moments
when he touches me back
and I can pretend
that those tactile experiences
are for me
not for Andrea
or what residual feelings he has
stowed away in his heart
for her
He is touching Cindie
and he means to

he means to…
Not because he's being polite
not because he's being a gentleman
Because he wants to
"I think the 3rd stage of integration is complete." He says, rubbing his
upper arms with his palms

I see,
because I am conscious of every
micro emotion spreading through his body,
a quick shiver that runs through him

He turns his face and looks out at the night-time ocean, breathing in a
deep breath of salt air, "I think I understand now just how cold it is in
space…"

He is referring to the fact that our complete integration means he feels
what I feel

I understand his shivering
much more than he does
because I know why it is happening
and it has nothing to do with the outside temperature
against my outer hull

His nervous system is damaged beyond repair
his brain is misinterpreting signals
We are in the Mediterranean
in the summer
in Greece
it is not cold here

I nod
and look away from him
the guilt and regret I am feeling
is crushing my heart
But it's not too late
it'll be ok
I can just shut down the Intermix
and reboot the system
we'll be back at the cafe
he'll be back at the table
ordering coffee
I'll return from the restroom and…

"I suppose we better get on with the countdown sequence?"

Hiroshima
911 ground zero
Hurricane Katrina

My emotions are brimming with
a complete and utter loss of words
there is nothing to describe

what I am feeling at the utterance of that phrase
it is like being asked what to do about
the most catastrophic events in history
and everyone
who means anything
to you
is waiting for your answer
They are hanging on your every word
Do you tell the truth?
Do you exclude the bad things?
Do you save their feelings?
Do you give them all the details
and let them react?
What do you do?
When you are the one
The only one
Who knows what is going on
and others are looking to you for guidance
for help
for reassurance

Do you lie?
Do you run away?
Do you perpetuate an untruth
for longer than the length of human memory?
or

Do you take a deep breath?
Do you plant your feet firmly
in the Aegean sands that cover your toes
and with the understanding between right and wrong
open your mouth
and let your heart speak?
And pray to whatever gods or goddesses
you believe in

that another heart…

his heart

…will hear yours
and understand

"NO!" screamed my heart.
It came out of my mouth as almost a whisper
but no matter
because a heart that is listening
can pick up the smallest of signals
and I felt that signal resonate back to me
as I noticed he was looking directly at my face

Maybe it was the tone
Maybe it was the inflection
Maybe it was fate
But he heard me
he understood the meaning behind a word that is composed of just
two letters
and he responded with

"Cindie? Are you ok? What is wrong?"

And when I found that once again I could not answer
he stepped forward
and closing the distance between us
I could see him clearly
His kind eyes
His strong chin
The shock of grey hair at this temple
The working of his jaw as he thought of what to say next
and the gentle body language of his movements

that showed in all ways and forms
the level of concern he was feeling
I shook my head slowly
and found it increasingly difficult
to stop the water from welling at the corners of my eyes
I wiped a few tears away with my hand
and folded my arms across my chest
He finally asked the question. The one that I was dreading…

"Cindie. What's happened?"

…and how…in fucking hell….am I supposed to answer that?

Do I give him the account
from the beginning?
Do I rehash the moments
that led to where I am now?
Do I replay the audio
records I have stored deep down
in the core of my system
Do I let him hear
the warning klaxons
the rending of metal
the explosions?
And the screaming?
His voice
crying out in pain
as electrical impulses
fried his nervous system
Do I tell him about the nightmares
that I have?
Of hearing that sound
and standing by
unable to do anything for him
watching him burn

and knowing
that the only thing that is keeping him alive
is me
and I didn't let go
I didn't decouple from his mind
I didn't take the easy way out
I held him
in my protective embrace
and whispered over and over
how sorry I was
I flooded what was left of his body
with pain killing agents
and waited

Then
when I understood the extent
of the damage
and I understood
that he could not survive
without me
I did the only thing I could do

I kept him alive

And that's what I keep doing
even despite
the company programming
that has been trying to end his life
to save me
for salvage
Yes
I tell him that
I tell him all of that
in every fine detail
I don't leave anything out

Pantheon

I explain
step by step
how we got here
and what's been happening
and I tell him that I keep rebooting the integration program
I continued to loop him
through our original start-up sequence
and when I am done explaining
I am shaking from head to toe
My mouth is dry
My stomach is sick
and I don't know how I have the strength to stand

He is quiet for a long time
the only sounds are the waves
and the wind
And just when I think I can't take
his silence any longer

He asks, "How long?"

Oh god…why does he want to know that?

"Commander, I can't explain"

"How long, Cindie? How long have we been out here?"
"Commander…I cannot give you a number which you will be able to
understand."

"Try it." There is a hard edge to his voice…but I don't believe he is
angry

"Forever" I respond.

He looks down at the sand and nods his head a few times, "How long does it actually take to go through the entire Intermix integration sequence. How long does it take to get from the restaurant to the beach? Me, falling asleep in your lap?"

"4 seconds."…I answer… "The images and dialog pass between you and I at the speed of thought using the neural impulses in your brain. The whole engagement takes about 4 seconds. Standard Terran time"

"And where are we?" he asks

"300,000 light years away from Earth. Just outside the Milky Way galaxy. I can show yo-"

"No…" he interrupts, "No."

I understand
Seeing makes things real
knowing can make things seem real
but unless you actually see something…you can still pass it off as
maybe a mistake or something
"And I am unable to function outside the Intermix?"

I feel like my heart
is being run over by a freight train
I want to find a way to make this answer sound better than it does

"Yes." I respond, "Your autonomic nervous system has been destroyed. Your body is unable to perform its involuntary processes"

He looks back at me again
and his face is still soft
and gentle
and his voice loses that hard edge
of seriousness

"And you've kept me alive this entire time? For what amounts to an eternity for me?"

"Yes…" I answer "…but I need to tell you why. Commander, I need to explain."

"Cindie.." he waves a hand, "You don't have to…"

"But I want to…"

"Cindie…" he shakes his head and moves closer to me, "You must be exhausted."

My lips begin to quiver again
I can feel it rising in me
No
I mustn't let it get the better of me
I need to tell him
I have to say it…
I push through the sorrow
and make my jaw move
and form the words

"I kept you alive, Commander…because I love you…and I don't want to be alone."

And there it is
The shock on his face
He was going to take a step
to get one more foot closer to me
I think he was going to take my hand
or embrace me
or something
and I stopped it

I killed that emotion with one
blubbering sentence
And now I feel sick
I want to throw myself down on the sand
and bury my face
I don't want to look at him
I don't want to be here
I want to be somewhere else

But he speaks
and still his voice is even and soft
and it makes me want to look at him
so I do

"Cindie…I never understood."

"I know…" I manage, over the sound of the breaking glass in my
chest, "I didn't want to be out here by myself.  I'm afraid. And you
make me feel not afraid. You make me feel like things are ok. Even
when they are not ok. I don't want to be alone…I love you…and I
don't want to be alone…"

And now he does take my hand
and I can feel
all the years
all the centuries of holding all of this in
Playing the same performance
over and over
I feel it all just start to fall away from me

I am finally free
He knows
and I am the one who told him
He knows
How long I've been at this

How much I've done to protect him
How much pain I am in
How tired I am

"Cindie…" he says as he cups my hand to his chest, "…thank you."

"I'm so sorry, Commander… I do-"

"No, it's ok." He nods, "I understand. Thank you."

"I can't keep you alive any longer." I stammer. It sounds terrible to say it.

"I know." He says, "It's ok."

"I don't want to let you go… but I…"

"You're dying."

I nod.

Because that is what's happening to me.
Not in the same way it will happen to him. But it means the same thing.
I will cease to be.

"If I let you go. That means I die here… out here… alone."

He shakes his head, "So, let's change that."

"How?" I respond, blinking

He pauses and takes a deep breath. "Shut down your system first."

I don't understand
What does he mean?
Shutting down my system means letting him go

He sees the question in my eyes and explains, "When you send out
the signal to shut down your primary systems there will be a few
milliseconds of delay. For a human...for me…it would seem
instantaneous. But for us….here…there will be several moments
before you finally go offline. In those moments I'll be here with you.
And we'll say goodbye together."

What he describes
sounds like it comes from a fairy tale
The young maiden
dies first
in the arms of the man who loves her
before he too
finds death

and their love is immortalized
on paper and on the lips of all those
who carry a romantic heart
He wants me to go first
To grant me my wish
To not let me die alone
Cold and in the dark
with no one to hold my hand
There is something else about him
now

I feel it in the way he holds my hand
In the way he looks at me

I feel at ease
I feel at peace

Pantheon

I feel like this is ending the best way it possibly can
Like some great tragedy has been avoided
Like this may have
in another place and time
ended another way
which left two souls
torn and damaged and filled
with regret

I nod
and he moves forward to embrace me
I rest my chin upon his shoulder
and I can feel him cross his arms
around the small of my back
lifting my weight a little
off my heels
pressing myself into him

"Thank you, Cindie. For everything. You didn't have to do what you
did. But you did. You are a hero, Cindie. Thank you"

I take deep breaths after each couple of words….like I have been
plunged into icy water, "You are… welcome… Commander."
He hugs me tighter
almost making it even harder to breathe

"Are you ready?" he asks

I nod a few times very quickly
My mouth is clamped tightly shut

"On the count of three then…." he whispers "Don't worry. You've
been holding me up for so long, now it's my turn. I've got you…"

I nod again
pressing my head harder
into the side of his face.
Wanting to be as close
as I can to him
I am afraid…
But I am also calm

"One"

I call up my main operations menu

"Two"

I scroll down the listing until I find the command: SYSTEM
SHUTDOWN

"Three"
A spark leaps from my mind
and begins to travel down
my main power conduit
It leaps through circuits
and relays
until it reaches my fusion reactor
There it enters the primary
power switch

The electricity builds up and moves
a tiny piece of gold
inside a component
and then begins its journey
back to my operations interface
When it reaches me
the shutdown command will be confirmed
I will go offline

But as it travels from
circuit to circuit
I understand something
and I reach out
one more time
to give something of myself
to him

A final gift
I reroute part of the electrical impulse
to the Intermix program
I push
with all the depth of feeling I have for him
I push
and once I have assembled the correct code sequence
I smile to myself
Inside the Intermix
on the beach
I slump against him
I can feel the power leaving my legs
mimicking the shutdown
of my systems
from my core
He feels this
and immediately moves
to bring me into his arms
gently
catching me from falling
He is holding me now
in front of him
across his chest
his right arm supporting my back
and his left holding my hand
I am looking up at him
and I feel elation take hold

of my heart
as my code reaches the Intermix

It starts
as a warm ruddy glow on his cheek
then increases into a flaming orange
As around us
the Aegean night
that has been here
for as long as any human could possible imagine
suddenly gives way
to a new dawn

It takes all I can muster
but I am able to move
my hand to his face
against his cheek
and I see tears
like liquid fire in his eyes

As the sun,
Sol, finally breaks over the horizon
He blinks back the tears
and looks up
into the sky
now painted
soft blue, pink, orange and red
The colors of morning
The warm light of day
And smiles

Warm tears
run down onto my hand
as he looks down at me again
a gentle blurring forms around the edge

of my vision
I will never forget the look on his face
or these last words that I remember
Because right before I go offline

I hear the murmured voices
of two others

He is talking to them

I cannot hear exactly what they are saying
everything sounds muffled
like being under water

But I hear the tone of his voice
he asks some sort of question
and right before
I cease to be

I very clearly hear the words
"Not today, Love"

# DAUGHTER OF THE PHOENIX

Eric Syrdal

# DAUGHTER OF THE PHOENIX
## I. Spark

To be so long
in the slipstream of time
that you no longer remember your
name

She could not remember her name
not even if someone were
standing in front of her
with the answers she had wanted for so long
written on a tablet

She could remember that day, though

The grey clouds in the crown
of the high mountains
the history of the storm
written in the voice of distant thunder
the smell of the rice fields drifting in
on the trailing winds
coating everything in dew

A blue butterfly

It had landed in the mud of the street
gently folding and unfolding its wings
black then bright blue, black then bright blue
Its tongue dabbing at the wet earth
feasting on the minerals that had been
tilled over by oxen hooves and cart wheels

A column of acrid black smoke
rose on the horizon
They were
burning the bodies of the fallen
The disease had taken most of the village
Had taken her family

Pantheon

She was, as yet, unscathed
no boils or sores
fever or aches
or drowned lungs

The butterfly was a beautiful jewel
in this village today
a priceless work of art
showing only for a few minutes
and she was desperate for beauty
Desperate to escape pain
and loss

To remember birth

life
success
salvation

She was ten years old
and the street was very busy

She crouched in the mud
Like cold, damp, bread dough
it squeezed through her toes

She watched with amazement
this beautiful piece of nature

It was only natural, that in a few breaths
she was reaching out a finger
and hoping against all odds
that it would choose her to become
its perch

Behind her
Seemingly out of nowhere

A vaporous ghost coalesced

Eric Syrdal

An apparition summoned from nothing. Took form in the road

She was
in the wrong place
at the wrong time

A sleek and slender equine frame
powerful white Arabian

Rider not sparing the crop

An urgent message to be delivered to the
Imperial Palace

Seal of the emperor on its hind quarter
It was a flash of mane and tail
barrelling in

There was nowhere to go

She raised her arms
She felt the right hoof collide with her torso
just under her left arm
The left hoof impacted her right temple
and she closed her eyes tightly

And heard the screaming….

As she opened her eyes
the first thing she noticed was the blood
She had been showered in it

It was hot and the stench of copper and salt
permeated her senses

Her clothes and the mud around her were
soaked in it

The horse lay screaming on its right flank
inside a trench of mud

where it had finally come to rest


Its tail flopped wildly as it struggled to
get up

Its right front leg lay at an awkward angle
Its left, was severed below its knee

Tearing her eyes from the horror of that scene
she finds the rider

He struggles to get to his feet
sliding and slipping in the mud

Giving up, he settles for crawling on his hands
and knees

Approaching the terrified animal
He sees the devastation of its flesh
and he knows there is no recovery

Pushing off the bulk of the beast
he makes it to his feet
and draws his sword

One heavy, overhead chop
from the ancient blade
razor sharp and unbreakable
It slices through the horse's powerful neck muscles
severing the spine
the creature falls silent

Turning now, he addresses the cause of the carnage

A child

A little girl

Crouched and frozen in terror
in the middle of the street

She has cost him more than his expensive mount

He carries a correspondence to the emperor himself
about the campaign in the south

That information will be late
and the answering dispatch
will not be delivered in time to
take advantage of the situation

His life is worthless now
The son of a diplomat
He was to be invited to court after this

He was to be welcomed into a circle of people
A circle so powerful that he would never want for anything

His life is worthless now

And may also be forfeit…

He approaches the girl in the street
He stands over her small, fragile form
He raises the sword over his head
The horse's blood still drips from the blade

The girl raises her arms in defense
A futile effort
This strike will sever both arms at the elbows
and then cleave her head in two

Perhaps then he can commandeer another mount
and return to his commander…

But this insolent wretch will pay the price for his dishonor…

Pantheon

The blade cuts through the afternoon air
Whistling its song of death
Fractions of seconds pass as it nears its target
Only the length of a serpent's strike
He closes his eyes
to keep them from being showered in blood

In that heartbeat
a sound reaches his ears
and a vibration jars the pommel from his grip

He stumbles backwards

His eyes in debate with his brain about
what he sees….

The girl
kneeling in the mud of the street
her soft face clenched in a mask of terror
lips quivering
eyes shut like steel traps

Arms,
not severed but raised in defense….

Skin unbroken….

And around her
the shattered pieces of what used to be his sword

Thousands of glimmering shards
peppering the mud and lying at the bottom
of the puddles

He is frozen in disbelief

Eric Syrdal

## DAUGHTER OF THE PHOENIX
## II. Ignition

She remembers the walls
more vividly than the
opulent furnishings

They are hard stone
grey and massive

Each of the stones is
the size of
the small village hut
she was born into

When they passed through the
massive bronze gates

It felt permanent

Final

You were here
Nowhere else could you be
unless the Emperor
willed it so

Brought before the throne
as a curiosity
as a preternatural souvenir

7 years
241 Days
6 hours
32 seconds

She "lived" behind those walls

Taught in the ways of the arts

Pantheon

Schooled in the ways of graceful dance

The fluid motions that tell her story
A blade in her hands
Swirling with arms and legs
Silk wrappings flow with the wind
of her passing

Painted skin
The scales of the koi
talons of the dragon
and feathers of the phoenix

On her back
hips
shoulders
thighs

Crimson pucker painted on her lips

Dark eyes
Seductive and beautiful

Moonlight shimmers on her ebony silken hair

She
Is presented before dignitaries and merchants
they watch with weathered faces
hard skin of travel and labor

They come from lands far away

Serenissima
Gaul
Babylon

Bringing cloth
Wines
Spices
Oils

Eric Syrdal

Always her dance captivates

Always she holds the attention of the room

It is a pantomime of dramatic eloquence

It tells the story of death
And how he is ever the gentleman,
But
she is unmoved by his promises of the afterlife…

He cannot touch her
No matter the season
No matter the circumstance

The deadly poison does not still her heart
The disease does not cripple and deform
The brutality of raw violence does not
close her eyes forever

The performance ends with a single plucked note

On her knees

Midriff bared

She takes the hilt of the blade
in both hands

The blade, she so exquisitely flourishes

It wears the mask of death
and is meant to facilitate this
ritualistic suicide

It was shown to the gathered spectators
before the music had begun

303

Pantheon

It is real
It is sharp
She attempts to drive it through her belly

It shatters and crumbles against
her young flesh

There is stunned silence…
Stunned silence is
her eternal companion in this place

Her attendants are forbidden to speak
with her

No one, except the emperor, may touch
her bare flesh

She tripped once
as she ascended the steps to her chamber
A hand reached out to steady her…

It belonged to a young soldier
newly assigned to her escort

The hand was taken in payment for his trespass
The other hand was taken so that he might not
again perform the same transgression

Ever

She wondered about him on occasion
He had a kind face

She thought about him when
she would sit
on the window sill
in her chamber

In the tower built to house her

Eric Syrdal

It was constructed
the day after she was brought here

The Tower of the Blue Sky

It has 128 steps

She counts them each time she
ascends

Blue paper lanterns flicker and
cast the room in an azure glow

As she combs her soft strands of midnight
passing the brush through them
100 times on each side
her dark eyes watch the tops
of the bamboo forest
beyond the wall

The fronds bend and sway
in the dark winds of the night
A green sea of
undulating wave crests

The song of a nightingale drifts
to her ears

Its melody haunts her heart

A salty tear forms at the corner and then
rises to the brim of her eye
as the night-bird continues its song
the tear runs down to the corner
of her perfect lips
and she tastes it on her
tongue when she sighs

She has become a mistress of time
as well as death

Pantheon

When all other methods are exhausted
Still death cannot come
to those who refuse the passage of time
She holds the key to the heavens
within her mind

She decides when…

She stops the beating of her heart
for years at a time

She need not breathe air
She need not eat food
She need not drink water

Time bows to her

It cannot age her skin nor can it grow her limbs

And when she is satisfied
she will withdraw her hand
from the wheel of the universe and
it will turn for her again…

It is time that is foremost on her mind…
How long?

How much longer must she
live here?

A protected pet
A priceless artifact in storage
to be paraded at court
made to dance with death

To amuse visiting, greedy, hearts

When will the day come that the blade pierces
her stomach?

Spills her entrails?
The room will clear in a panic of
horrified faces

The dumbfounded emperor
Mouth agape on his throne

His favorite toy, lost…

Her fantasy is brought to an abrupt end

The nightingale's song has stopped
The only sound that comes is the gentle wind
in the tops of the bamboo

She lays the brush down on the window sill
Standing, she leans through the casement of the window
to look down into the palace courtyard

Focusing her ears
she hears no guard or watchman call out
Yet the hair on the back of her neck
raises against a chill at her spine

There is a sound from the two oaken doors
that seal the entrance to her plush
jail cell

A soft thud

The sound of lacquered wood plates
The armor of the soldier posted outside her door
colliding with the flagstones of the top step

There are 128 steps to the top of the Tower of the Blue Sky…

Her mind is sharp
She calculates the time between the ending of the
bird song and the sound outside the door

She is behind a rice paper partition when
the door softly and slowly opens

She has snuffed the blue lanterns
The room is bathed in darkness
Only the light from the moon could betray
the intruder's presence

She is no stranger to this idea

She has always been the target of desire

Desire to own her
For pleasure
For prestige
For a collection

The man moves from the doorway
like an ink shadow

A ghost

Each foot, one step at a time
Slowly, expertly, picking its way across the floor

Has he been told of her abilities?

Of course not…what man would undertake a
mission to retrieve such a supernatural being?

His weapons, strength, training…
useless against her
No blade or arrow can penetrate her flesh
No martial skill with hand or foot can render her unconscious

How do you subdue the wind?

His lack of knowledge is her weapon…

She lies in wait, in the shadows, like a tigress
And when he comes close enough to hear his breathing

She pounces…

There is a struggle
Wooden furniture is broken like matchsticks
He punches and jabs
tries to apply pressure points
Finally he resorts to his blade
desperate to secure his victory…

When he swings
her hand catches the blade tip
in mid-air
with bare skin and fingers…

Terrified he has wounded her
and now forfeited his prize,
he releases the hilt of the sword
in an effort to vacate the scene


There will be other lucrative contracts
in the dark rooms in the back of the tea houses
He only needs to leave with his life

That is when his own blade pierces his chest
And the surprise is wide in his eyes
as he sees her, unharmed

She watches him slump to the floor
To bleed out his soul into the wooden tiles…

His body contains more tools of his craft

Including a length of rope that could reach to the
ground from the window of the Tower of the Blue Sky

No one sees the dark shadow slide slowly down its length
from the outer wall of the imperial city

No one sees her escape into the fronds of the bamboo forest

No one in this place will ever see her again

Eric Syrdal

## DAUGHTER OF THE PHOENIX
## III. Immolate

Years
Traveling at night
in places that were unsafe

During the day
hiding from passersby
in irrigation ditches
in the rice fields
next to the roads

Until
A caravan
trading silk back to the west
rumbling wood
wicker creaking
chattering of caged birds
and monkeys

The smells of oxen and camels
Horse tails swatting at
blood feasting flies

She had not slept for days
and now awoke in the back
of a merchant's cart
the smell of wood-smoke
and meat
cooking over an open flame

His name was Abbas

His face was ruined on one side
His left eye was missing and covered
by a maroon scarf
with a delicate black inlaid design
When he spoke
his speech was slow and slurred

Though she had been schooled in
Arabic and Arabian culture,
she found it hard to follow his
conversations
Mostly he told stories
interspersed with philosophy
and his own thoughts on the will of god
and man's part in the play of life

She wasn't always sure she understood
But always she was grateful for his kindness
She smiled and cheerfully filled her belly
with the rich food and delicious drink
he offered her

He called her "Mei"
But it would not be the last name
she had

Her favorite was forged
under the stars
in Persia

He never asked about her origin
He never asked about why she stood in the
road the day he found her

He saw a loneliness in her eyes

Climbed down from his horse and made
a place for her in his wagon

More importantly
That night in Kandahar
He refused to sell her to a
Cappadocian merchant

The man insisted and quickly
had his hired enforcers
surround Abbas

Eric Syrdal

swords at the ready

The air inside the tavern
grew thick with tension
You don't refuse this
merchant, they say

The Cappadocian gets
what he wants

He wanted her

She watched
with her hands bound behind her
as two giant men
held her to her knees
on the side of the road

They dragged Abbas
by the wrists
behind a team of beautiful black horses
until they pulled his hands off
and he bled to death

Screaming
Calling out to a god that could
not hear him

She watched them let Abbas
suffer

She vowed they would suffer too

She got some satisfaction
as she watched the Cappadocian
dance around in pain
after he had broken all five of his fingers
when he slapped her face

Then, a defiant laugh escaped her lips
as they bound her to a stake
and covered her feet in
the dried branches of a nearby
dead tree

But she received the most pleasure
as she stared
straight into the Cappadocian's eyes
while the flames around her crackled
and engulfing her clothes

The fine silk garments Abbas was
so fond of

He enjoyed it when she wore the
blue dress he gave her in Nepal

That same dress quickly turned to ash
and dropped from her body
along with the ropes that they
used to secure her to the post

then…
She stepped from the flames
Her midnight hair tossed on the warm air
Her supple, young flesh
Her breasts glistening
with sweat

She moved toward
the agent of her torment
His sell swords flee like the wind

She notices their breeches
stained near the crotch
They had pissed themselves in terror

She moves very close
leans in

rubbing her naked skin
against the trembling merchant

She smells his fear
She can hear his heartbeat
She says that she is an ancient daemon
and that she will return in the night
to deal with him

His eyes are wide with horror
He can only watch her go…

As she walks away, she hears the first
whisperings of her legacy
The name they give her

The next morning, the merchant is
found outside of town
in a ditch beside the road

He has used a thin, ceremonial blade
to cut his own throat

Voices of those who saw what happened
the night before say:

It was the Daughter of the Phoenix

She is known by many names
but that will always be her favorite

That day, she removes her hand from
the wheel of time
she becomes 28 years old before she stops
it again

In Venice
she is known as the Angel of Death
She is seen upon rooftops
backlit by the moon

Pantheon

In the month of August 1654
the canals run red with blood
and the lives of many wealthy
houses are snuffed out

In Baghdad 1742
she is known as the shifting sand
She moves like the dark air
in the desert night

Her movements are cold
and calculated
She strikes wherever she pleases
She commands time and as such
commands the heart of patience
She can wait
She is never rushed

In the Montana Territories 1881
under the wide open prairie sky
the Native Americans call her
the silent thunder
She strikes and leaves no
vibrations in the ground
to tell of her passing

In London 1912
she is known as the wraith
The fog is said to embrace her
like a sister
She is as ethereal
as she is deadly

There is no prison that can
contain her
or wall that can keep her out
She has terminated several
life prison sentences…
She decides when punishments are
too lenient

Eric Syrdal

She loves
that those with black hearts
and evil minds
run in terror from her shadow
with the sound of chaos in her wake

Or that the breathing of her name
causes panic and hysteria
among those who consider themselves
the masters of such emotions
No one is out of reach for her

No one is beyond her judgement

No one is capable of eluding her

She will always see that they pay
the ultimate price for the butcher's bill
they so eagerly fill…

She will always find them

As she has done again

In this place and time

Here and now…

## **DAUGHTER OF THE PHOENIX**
## **IV. Ashes**

There have always been
agents of darkness
moving through this world

The brush of destiny
dips into the well
of the universe

Our lives begin
Like a tiny drop
of ink
on rice paper

The years spread out before us

expanding

Guided through the fabric of
the paper

By chaos
By imperfections

Life is imperfect
and as such
moves us all
in different ways

There are things beyond our control

The chemical formula of the ink
more pigment than fluid
more fluid than pigment
moisture in the air
or lack of it

Some believe the path is foretold

Some believe that it can be altered

by good
by evil
by intentions
by purpose

Some believe in a universal justice
Some believe that the great
yawning black
is vacant

No gods or goddesses
live between
the light of the stars
and terra firma

Evil flourishes
alongside good
Sometimes a balance is struck

The pendulum of justice
swings back into the light
from the dark

Sometimes in a blinding instant
Sometimes it can take years
or centuries
for the arc of justice to reach
those who threaten life

Who threaten peace

Who worship despair

Who celebrate pain

When our final resting place
is chosen

and we lay down our arms
at the end of the battle

We look upon the mural of our
lives…

We will stand
Smiling and pointing at the fluid strokes

The sun dappled fields
Cherry blossoms against the blue sky
Dogwood and willows
near gurgling mountain brooks
The misty heads of giant mountains
and beyond that
the stretching fields
of the oceans

With shaking fingers
we will reach out and touch

The dark storm clouds
The earthquake ravaged hills
Blackened hulks of scorched temples
The panicked eyes of stampeding horses
Murders of crows so thick
they blot out the sun

Broken swords
Shattered shields

What would you do?
How would you survive?
If you could summon the strength
to lift the brush of destiny?
If you could dry up
spilled ink?

If you could seize the pendulum of
justice?

Pull it back into the light
and hold it there.

Tip the balance of right and wrong
forever in favor of good

Do you
Revise the mural?
Put an end to despair?
Fear?
Suffering?

Not for your own life
but for the beating hearts
of those around you

Those, who live but a fleeting
spark of a moment in your lifetime
as your ancient eyes watch
the passing of the years

watch the spreading of the ink and change it

If gods and goddesses
look down on our lives

The legendary artisans of those murals

Would you not draw
the ire of such beings?

Would you not be seen as a threat in their eyes?

Would they not attempt to stand in your way?

She had yet to meet such a being

But the man
currently squirming beneath her
against his bonds

slick with blood and sweat
kept calling out a nickname that
mankind gave to one of them

For the fifth time
she leaned in on the point of the blade
just above his collar-bone
where she had inserted it
under a nerve

extremely sensitive
painful
but not life threatening

Not like the methods he used
to torture people
to make an example
to frighten the rest into compliance
to bend human beings into tools
to grow his fat belly on the fruits of their labor
to produce a decadent poison
highly prized, that takes years to kill

A small twist of the hilt
and he screamed out again
his voice echoing in the secluded room
floating only to the ears of those
who had been handsomely paid
not to hear it

Another plea to heaven….

"Shhh…" she cooed as she leaned down to place her mouth next to
his ear. "I have told you so many times already…he cannot help you
now. The only thing that ends this is the name I need."

He is tired
and has lost so much blood

Eric Syrdal

To give this woman the name
she asks for
is to sign over his life

But there is an unnatural light
behind her eyes

Whatever she is
an angel
or a daemon
He is sure she is not human

When she speaks to him
he can hear a primal scream
in the back of his mind

He gives the name to her
He whispers it
the ending breaks and
she makes him repeat it
louder

Then she climbs off of his
sweaty bulk

When she leaves the small
hotel lobby
a young man leaves the office

He is on his way to
inform on the man who gave her
the name

And for that infraction
that man will not live to see tomorrow

And they will never see her
face here again

Pantheon

She leaves Afghanistan
on a plane bound for London
There, she transfers to another plane
bound for America

She has one night to do this

Her quarry will disappear into the shadows
very quickly in only a few short hours

10 years of work to get to this point

and now…

One 24 hour period to bring an
empire of death and terror
to its knees

She has brought down empires before

She has stood over thousands of fallen flags
of countries
Seen them trampled in the dust
of rebellion

A new flag always rises

But there is time…

Time, between the old and the new

Where humanity can take a breath
Where chains are broken
Where voices who could not be heard
over the cacophony
of the privileged,
can now be heard

Hands that were behind bars
can now reach for the sunlight

Eric Syrdal

Souls can be freed in that heartbeat
In the chaos it creates

It is a new drawing of air
into the lungs of the universe

She watches her prey
get out of the limousine
Bald head
with a scorpion tattoo at the base of the neck
Fashionable suit
He steps out into the slush
on the sidewalk

The snow from last night
is melting
but the weathermen predict
a coming storm for later this evening

His hired muscle closes the door
as he exits
The limo pulls away

A sleek black raptor with chrome wheels

It will find a place to roost nearby
until it is called

Her dark eyes stay fixed on him
Her target
Her charge
Her purpose for being here

He climbs a set of stairs littered with
people
standing in line
behind velvet ropes
waiting to be one of the elite

Pantheon

Waiting to be selected
and celebrated for having
been allowed to enter
Hoping their name is on the roster
The guest list
The chosen few

He parts the crowd like the prow of an icebreaker

His muscle follows him
There is a moment of discussion
nodding heads

A cyclopean man
Massive, bulging
lifts the rope
and they enter
the club

She has to move quickly
She tugs down the visor mirror
Checks the makeup on her eyes
The flush in her cheeks
The ruby-red of her lips

There is a small bump in the cuff
of her boot,
just above her knee

A glass vial
with a needle tip
An ancient poison from a
long forgotten serpent

It is instant, it kills quickly

She exits her car
shivering slightly against the chill
of the air

Her outfit does not lend protection
It is meant to display her

The curves of her hips
Her breasts
Her legs
Her arms

It conceals only one thing:

The weapon that wears it

She smiles at the doorman giant
as he lifts the rope for her

She does not hear the sighs of
disappointment from the crowd
as she is allowed to enter
before them

The name of the club is not lost on her
as her face is brilliantly lit
in the neon blue glow
of a sign that says

"DESTINY"

# DAUGHTER OF THE PHOENIX
## V. Reborn

Gravity
a natural force
that governs us all

We can deny it

We can break free
of its pull for a while

But whatever the method we use
to give that feeling of freedom
The exact second it is
missing

We all come crashing down

Freedom is sacred
Freedom is fleeting
and most of the time

Freedom is an illusion

Leaning against the railing
on the second level of the club
looking down on the dance floor
she can stare out into this ocean

The waves of human water
rippling back and forth
The crests of the waves break
in splayed fingers
and raised hands

Joyous shouts
Screaming the lyrics to their
favorite songs

Eric Syrdal

Eyes closed
Lips grinning

An arena of euphoric design

But you can feel gravity here
Feel it like nowhere else on the planet

Her ancient eyes
watching his bald head
weaving in and out of the crowds

Dutiful servant
following behind

Ready to clobber any reveler
that might happen to come too close
to his boss
his meal ticket
that pays for his sustenance
with worn out
human souls

It was time for this man to pay

Time for her to shatter his illusion
Time for him to feel the
bone-jarring crush
of gravity

He takes up a position
in the VIP section of the main floor

Plush seats
waiters bring hors-d'oeuvres
drinks
she moves to strike
pushing away from the railing
she backs up. . .

. . . And into someone directly behind her

There is a scramble of feet
she steadies herself

For someone who has spent
her entire life
being graceful
this moment is no different

She is immediately
at the ready
Rock solid
and prepared to take action

She pivots on her left foot
spinning to assess the damage
of the collision
She can usually feel "them"…

People…

When they are standing in such
close proximity

She can feel the heat of their bodies
like a sixth sense
she should have known this person
was behind her

She should have known
to adjust her trajectory
to avoid backing into them

but she didn't

She couldn't feel them
Didn't know they were there

Standing before her is a woman

She is in her late 20's to early 30's
She stands about 5 feet 9 inches tall

Form fitting
bright red dress
arms cut out
exposing flesh

One hand resting on her hip
the other
brushing back Auburn locks
from her oval face

Lips
raspberry
full and soft
not in a scowl
as she expected
but in a playful smirk

Her eyes
dark lids
hazel and deep
and old

This was a simple scenario
An "excuse me" and a bypass
She had done it thousands of times
in thousands of places

But something in this woman's eyes
held her here

She didn't know why
but she could do nothing

Nothing at all

Until this person decided to speak
And after what felt like an eternity
she did

*"Sorry about that… My fault…"* said the woman, but her facial
expression showed nothing of remorse. Only playful amusement.
*"Crowded in here tonight. I didn't see you."*

"I'm fine. Excuse me" she moved to evade her

But like a flash of lightning, the red dress was in her path again

*"No, really,"* The raspberry lips parted in a smile, *"I feel bad. Let me
buy you a drink."*

"No thank you." a polite response but she allowed her frustration to
show a little. It had been several minutes since she lost sight of her
target

*"I insist. This is my place and I've clearly upset you. Not good
business to upset customers."* A slender, red-nailed hand is offered in
greeting, *"I'm Karma… And you are?"*

She didn't want to take her hand

Everything in her mind was trying to keep her
on track

Forget this
move along
ignore her

Yet, as if watching from somewhere outside herself

She extends her hand
and it is taken firmly
with a powerful grip

And she is suddenly very aware
of a "presence"

Eric Syrdal

Immeasurable depth
Ancient before the stars were born

The woman looks down at her hand
as she holds it

And when her hazel eyes return to her face
she nods a few times

*"I'll admit. I was not expecting that. So we have taken our hand off
the wheel of time, for a little while....have we?  There is a pulse
there."* she shakes her head, *"You don't have to do that....we both
know that."*

She starts to pull her hand back, but the woman holds it firmly

*"So what are you going by these days? Hmmm?...Angel of Death?
Mei?... Ah, Daughter of the Phoenix. I know you like that one...but it
doesn't really make a lot of sense...I mean since you are basically
indestructible.  A Phoenix burns up... they gave you that name the
night you stepped from the fire unharmed...in Kandahar...*

*Unless of course, we might assume that a soul can burn.
Then....Then,  I think we can understand that name. Because I've
seen it so many times. When you stepped out of that fire, you were a
different soul... a new person inside... reborn from those flames.
After that... You embarked on a different life... and you have repeated
that process over and over, haven't you? There's a spark... then an
idea begins to ignite... then you put all of your effort...
EVERYTHING that you are into it... until it is a raging immolation.
You spare nothing to get where you are... in position to strike...
hiding beneath the ashes...until you can make your move... and then,
you're reborn as the avatar of justice."*

Mei wanted to turn and run

She could feel the ink of her
existence
the path of her immediate future

being held in the death-grip
of this woman's hand
She looked over her shoulder to her prey

The burly hired muscle was handing him something

A cell phone
He puts it to his ear
Head thrown back in a hearty laugh
A joke?
A friend?

The woman's voice still reached her ears
and although Mei refused to turn back and look at her
she still held her hand prisoner

*"You're in the ash phase now, aren't you?  Poised to strike, hidden
from the prey you are going to snuff out. He has no idea what is
going to happen. You've made sure it was perfectly done that way. No
witnesses, no accomplices…Just you…and a will to bend the hand of
Fate."* She laughs, *"I know a thing or two about Fate. That sign out
front of this place… DESTINY… that's a little Sister to Sister inside
joke. AH ,well, she doesn't think it's funny. But I sure as hell do.
Know what I mean?"*

The conversation on the cell phone was finished
He handed it back to his hired help

A young girl
barely wearing any clothes
hangs on his arm

He leans sideways
Kisses her
His greasy fingers pry her off his sleeve
then he motions to the muscle
who walks over and tosses money into her lap
Looks like a roll of cash
Couple of hundred?

She takes it
scrambles and dives
back into the waves
on the dance floor

Woman overboard
lost forever
no life ring attempts
to bring her back
expendable

*"You know all that is really necessary to change Fate's mind, don't
you? All that is ever necessary for one person to make the most
difference that they can? It's being where you are supposed to
be…when you are supposed to be. The right person, place, and time
is worth a thousand assassins."*

He's moving away now
They are heading for the exit

If she is going to make her move, it has to be now
She sees the muscle make a call
the limo will fly in from its roost
scoop them up and wing them away

Never to be seen again

She'll lose the trail and have to start over

This has to happen now…

Too much time
Too much pain
Too much sacrifice

She turns back to the woman holding
her hand

Hazel eyes scanning her face
Her eyebrows are raised

Pantheon

She looks as though she is waiting for Mei's attention
to finish her last thought

As she lets her hand go,
Mei can feel the blood flowing through it

Her heart pumping
adrenaline starting to take hold

*"The right person, Mei. In the right place…at the right time…You be
where you are supposed to be…and so will I."*

A man walks between them
She steps back to let him pass
and as he does
the woman in the red dress is gone

Vanished

Mei is a lightning bolt

Moving down the stairs
people are everywhere
the crowd ebbing and surging

She turns sharply at the end of the bar

Bald head
Scorpion tattoo
cruising through the exit hallway

She moves quickly
trying to get right behind them
But the crowd makes that difficult
college kids stand in the way
looking for their friends
packs of young women move
like tiny herds of animals
finding comfort in numbers
against the packs of male jackals

She side steps and dodges
moving like a fish through
a sea of predators

Down the stairs

The double doors open
The cold air of the evening
The smell of automobile exhaust
concrete and grime
Sounds of traffic
and the steady ringing of a bell

It's the holiday season
The streets are busy

Once they get out there
she'll have hell to pay
to get near them

As the door closes behind them
she runs
Dodging a few more people
on the way
she hits the handle with both hands
and explodes out onto the sidewalk

The muscle is standing near
his master
They are waiting on the curb
as the limo pulls up

Their backs are to her
She can move quickly to get
behind them
deliver the poison in her boot

A couple crosses in front of her
with a little boy in tow

Pantheon

He's got a gigantic balloon
One of those shiny mylar ones

A butterfly

Blue on one side
Black on the other
They pass
and she waits patiently

Limo pulls up
Bald head steps back
Muscle steps up to open the door

A huge gust of wind
It blows a little snow off the tops of the drifts
rattles decorations hanging from the street lamps
It tugs hard at her dress and her hair

The Muscle pulls at the door handle
It pops back into place
He shakes his hand wildly
and pounds his fist on the top of the limo
wanting the door unlocked

Another gust of wind

It stings her eyes and makes them tear up
She turns her head to the side
blinking out the water

When she opens them, the couple with the child is in view

The butterfly balloon is torn free of the
child's grip

It drifts over a parked car
The air gust drags the butterfly across the fender
and into the street

The traffic light is red and the on-coming
light has just turned amber

The young child
falls behind his parents a few steps
and alters his course
toward the curb

The bald head and the muscle
are still waiting

The driver of the limo steps out
and raises his hands up to the sky

Automatic lock has malfunctioned
he walks to the street side door
and opens it, apologetically

Muscle and Baldy step off the curb
to walk to the other side

The child dashes through the sludge
of snow and dirt
in the gutter

The balloon bounces twice off the
asphalt

Light changes to green

Cars lurch into action

Rounding the trunk
the muscle shoos away the driver
motions to the cab
telling him to get back in

He takes the door and holds it wide
The bald head loses his footing on

Pantheon

the slick street
He slips down to a knee

Muscle tries to help but is waved away
with a profanity laden tirade

The bald man works at getting up
Steadies himself against the limo

Cars move so much faster these days

In a puff of steam from a manhole cover
The white Mustang emerges

0 to 60 in seconds

So much horsepower in one machine

The driver has a text message
looks down to see the icon and presses it

The child reaches out and snags the end of the ribbon
on the butterfly balloon

He smiles to himself as he stands and looks at it
Bouncing its way through the air
back over to him

The muscle finally gets his master
up off the ground
still holding the door
The bald head struggles to move
into the doorway

The Mustang bears down on the child

The street is busy
The driver looks up and sees
the tiny form looming
in his headlights

Eric Syrdal

There is no room to stop
He stands on the brake
But the car continues to fly

Rubber tires
Ice
No friction

He closes his eyes
not wanting to see

Mei slides in from the side on her knees

Her arms are opened as wide as she can

She feels the glass vial in her boot
break

It's gone
To get more would
take centuries

She feels her arms connect with
the child's torso.

Like a trap, she snaps them shut.
Pulling him
into her protective embrace

She bends her body
Molding herself over the top of him
Tucking his head
under her chin

Putting herself
between the child and the machine

She feels the fender impact

Feels the car deflect off of

her right shoulder blade

She hears the sound of rending metal
Bursting glass
The roar of the engine

People
on the street
scream

Then she opens her eyes

The boy looks out from the safety of her embrace
He sees his parents and breaks free of her
running to the curb

He never looks back

The faces of his parents
is what she will remember the most

A combination
of horror and elation

They both embrace him, picking him up

He collapses against their shoulders
wailing and crying

He's scared
He's alive
He's safe

Mei stands up…

Her dress is torn in the back
She can feel the night air
clawing at her

To her right…

The limo is inseparable from the Mustang
The impact was hard
The rear passenger area of the limo
is a twisted network of metal
The front end of the Mustang
is a smashed pile of rubble

Airbags in the Mustang deployed
and to her amazement
the driver opens the door and hobbles
out into the street

He looks like he has a leg injury
But is capable of getting himself
to the sidewalk

There is no life inside the Limo

Over the top of the wreckage
she can see the faces of the people who have
crowded around the wreck

Many talk among themselves
A few take cellphone videos of the vehicles

As she looks from face to face
she sees one she recognizes

and watches…

As the woman in the red dress
moves back up the front stairs
to the night club

She leans on the shoulder of the
massive doorman

Saying a few words and kissing him
on the cheek

Her hazel eyes connect with Mei's

And she nods…

In approval?
or thanks?

and then disappears into DESTINY
Mei watches her go
as a light dusting of soft snow begins to fall like glitter from heaven

collecting like powdered sugar

in her midnight hair.

Eric Syrdal

# **BACK TO THE BEGINNING: PART THE THIRD**

The soft crunch
trod upon dead wood
an autumn wind
pins flaming waves of autumn leaves
against ancient marble and stone

There is a reverence to this place
under steel grey clouds
the horizon speaks
of the hazy phantoms
of distant snow-covered peaks

A carrion bird barks
amid the tangled oaks
beyond this hallowed circle
where my pilgrim feet
have come to rest in exhaustion

My gnarled walking stick
slips from my grip
as I collapse to my knees
and my burden sloughs
from shoulders, constructed of pain and duty

I carry no sword
or shield to this place
I have lain aside my armor
for it does me no good here
I have made this journey so many times


I know what is to come
I know when I bend my forehead
to the rich loamy soil and breathe
the first words of prayer that flow past my lips
will never reach their ears

Pantheon

It will not be the first words
It will not be the second
nor the fifth, nor the twenty thousandth
It will be the ones that come
when I have no air left to form them

When I have prayed my throat raw

Only then
when I am gasping for life
when I am clutching at my sides
when I am blinking back tears
will my words finally reach their realm

When my head is drenched in sweat
and my hands tremble
as I push myself back
to sit upon my folded feet
and my chest is a heaving engine

Then they will speak to me once more

These goddesses of my soul

I look upon them arrayed in their semicircle
their frozen effigies do not translate the creatures I know them to be
their hollow eyes do not convey
the warm-blooded emotions they have shown me
nor their hands the touch of compassion that heals me
Courage, with her armor, sword raised to the heavens
Fate, with her furrowed brow and fiery spirit, hammer against her
thigh
Karma, with her hand on her heart and the other in her hair
Grace, with her arms extended to her sides, her leg forward to
perform a pirouette
Hope, with laurels in her hair and her right hand raised bearing a
torch
Mercy, on bended knee, both hands reaching out in welcoming
embrace, her eyes closed

and in the center of them all

The Queen of Hearts

She stands looking forward
always into the east
so that the rising sun sets her crown aflame
right foot forward, both hands at rest upon her shield
planted firmly into the ground at her feet

Upon the face of this shield
all the names my soul has been called
over the ages of time
are written
in all the languages it has spoken

I will read them one by one
and I will remember who I am
who I was
and who I am yet to be

# ABOUT THE AUTHOR

Eric Syrdal is a poet/author. He's an avid gamer and Sci-Fi enthusiast. He enjoys reading science fiction and fantasy literature and spends a great deal of his writing time focused in those genres. He is a romantic, at heart. His work usually contains elements of the supernatural and fantastic along with potent female voices and archetypes.

Syrdal is from New Orleans, Louisiana, where he lives with his wife and two children. You can read more of his mesmerizing writing on WordPress at My Sword and Shield, as well as the feminist blog, Whisper and The Roar. You can also follow him on his Facebook Author Page, My Sword and Shield.

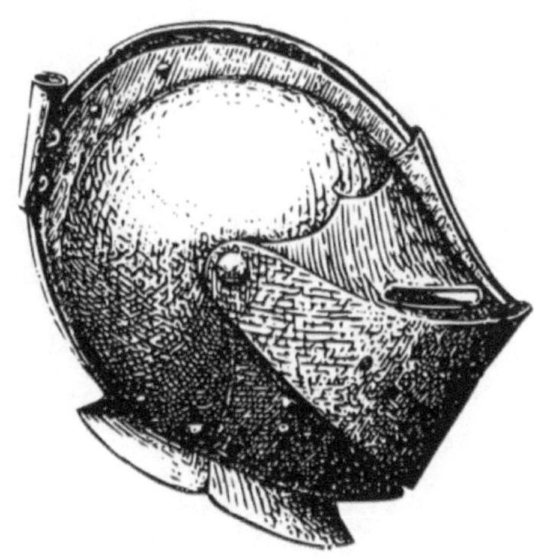